COACH NORTH

By the same author

WHISTLE AND I'LL COME
THE KID
STORM SOUTH
HOPKINSON AND THE DEVIL OF HATE
LEAVE THE DEAD BEHIND US
MARLEY'S EMPIRE
BOWERING'S BREAKWATER
SLADD'S EVIL
A TIME FOR SURVIVAL
POULTER'S PASSAGE
THE DAY OF THE COASTWATCH
MAN, LET'S GO ON
HALF A BAG OF STRINGER
THE GERMAN HELMET
THE OIL BASTARDS
PULL MY STRING

Featuring COMMANDER SHAW

GIBRALTAR ROAD
REDCAP
BLUEBOLT ONE
THE MAN FROM MOSCOW
WARMASTER
MOSCOW COACH
THE DEAD LINE
SKYPROBE
THE SCREAMING DEAD BALLOONS
THE BRIGHT RED BUSINESSMEN
THE ALL-PURPOSE BODIES
HARTINGER'S MOUSE
THIS DRAKOTNY

Featuring SIMON SHARD

CALL FOR SIMON SHARD

COACH NORTH

by Philip McCutchan

WALKER AND COMPANY
New York

Copyright © 1974 by Philip McCutchan

All rights reserved. No part of this book may be reproduced or transmitted in any form or by any means, electronic or mechanical, including photocopying, recording, or by any information storage and retrieval system, without permission in writing from the Publisher.
All the characters and events
portrayed in this story are fictitious.
First published in the United States of America
in 1975 by the Walker Publishing Company, Inc.

ISBN: 0-8027-5330-2

Library of Congress Catalog Card Number: 75-12187

Printed in the United States of America

10 9 8 7 6 5 4 3 2 1

1

LATE September sun glinting on blue and gold, the 31-seater touring car, pulling out from the Victoria coach station, turned left into Buckingham Palace Road. In the driving seat Frank Harkness, short, chubby, fair, thirty-five and married with two children, thought of home in Peckham as he watched the brake-lights of a grey Rolls in front of his bumper. Move a foot, stop, move another foot: London! London was okay, but not to drive in. The motorway was better, and after that, better still, the haul through Durham and Northumberland for the border and Scotland. It was a nomadic life for much of the time, but it suited Frank Harkness, a happy, smiling man who liked to be on the move even though he missed the wife and kids and usually suffered a touch of homesickness on the second day of the outward run.

Left turn for Ebury Street, move along it then left again for Grosvenor Place . . . right, left again—Park Lane. More Rollses—crises and cuts didn't seem to bother some people, they had all the spare money in the world—but good luck to them, Harkness thought. Halted at traffic lights, waiting, whistling, hand tapping on the wheel in time to the whistled tune, Frank Harkness pondered on the faces visible in his rear-view mirror: his charges, his companions, dependent upon him for all their wants for the next fourteen days. The lights changed, he went ahead for Marble Arch and into the Edgware Road. Another glance in the mirror: Harkness smiled, shook his head a little. That rear-view mirror glance almost always showed him a similar mixture, except when he was carrying a football crowd, or a club outing, both of which could be fairly bloody for a long-suffering driver when the beer cans came out. This lot, eager tourists, wouldn't be boozers, at any rate not en masse. They would be predictable in their aims, conformist in their composition: mostly middle-aged, some old, with only a sprinking of youth, worse luck—all keen to look, listen and learn. Three American Europe-doers—a smaller percentage than usual, was that—a Mr and Mrs MacFee, seeking their origins along with a daughter who somehow looked, to Harkness's experienced eye, divorced. Two French women, Mesdemoiselles Laffont and Libersart. A fat German woman on her own, Frau Borchardt. Otherwise, all British...

Stop, start—jam on the brakes... *Christ*! A quick look in the mirror again: they didn't seem ruffled. Frank Harkness went on whistling. A Scottish tune, *Will Ye No' Come Back Again*. If there was anything prophetic in that choice, it certainly failed to register with Frank Harkness, who saw no reason to doubt that he would be home on time.

* * *

Mark Graham looked sideways at the girl in the inside seat, feeling desire like a hot wave. Lovely silky hair—jet black—dimples, and a warm, soft mouth. Aware of that strong desire in his body, the girl nestled against Mark as the coach dragged its way through stale London air, hemmed in by taxis, cars, vans, buses and lorries, a press of metal that gave Frank Harkness an increased urge towards the freedom of the high roads north, past Amazonian female traffic wardens, whose yellow haloes sporadically spotted busy, hurrying pavement crowds. Jilly liked the crowd life: it meant—to her—gaiety and being part of things. She was an extrovert, gregarious: Mark was not. Scotland called Mark loud and clear—that, and being away on their own where desire, freed from the prying eyes of Jilly's mum and dad, could find its fruition in hotel bedrooms. Jilly, who as well as being gregarious was affectionate and wanted to please, had gone along wholeheartedly with the Scottish tour idea, though there had been a rearguard action, carried on more or less despairingly over many days, from Mum and Dad.

'It's not right. I'd never have been allowed to.' This was Mum, half in, half out of the small kitchen in Horsham.

'Your bad luck, Mum.'

'Don't be cheeky.' Reddening, Mum had vanished and started a clatter of saucepans. 'Your dad wouldn't have asked, what's more—'

'I'm going, Mum, so—'

'He wouldn't have respected me after—'

'Oh, that old-fashioned tripe—'

'It's not tripe, it's—it's *proper living*, Jilly. You've always been brought up properly. I don't understand you, really I don't.'

'I'm going, Mum.'

There had been a lot more from her father, when he'd got in from work, work being in an ironmonger's where Mr Ruff was next in line to the manager—honest, sober industry paid off, as he frequently said. With Jilly, he didn't cut a lot of ice. Stuffy, square like the little house in its patch of wattle-fenced garden. Protuberant eyes, weak chin, bald, forty-three. Mark Graham, who was tall and athletic—she giggled inside at the thought of that—with long, chestnut hair and what she considered a strong, romantic face, was bound to win and he did, hands down. Mr Ruff, given to talking a lot in a flat, monosyllabic voice and emphasizing important points with little jabs of a stubby forefinger, uttered unheeded warnings about primrose paths and coming to a bad end and—like Mum—not being respected. A load of cobblers! Jilly went out of the house with her head high the morning she left for Victoria, and met Mark in Horsham's Carfax for the London coach from Worthing. She was scarcely conscious of the forlorn, hopeless faces she left behind the gate as she banged it shut, though she did say, defiantly, lugging her handcase, 'Anybody'd think I wasn't ever coming back.'

* * *

In the next-to-rearmost pair of seats, near side of the coach, sat Ernie Peach and his wife Elsie. Ernie, just on sixty-one, had not long before received a twin pleasure, retirement from the London and South Coast Building Society, and the maturing of an endowment policy—just seven hundred and fifty quid. Not enough to do a lot with—not enough for a cruise for two in the sort of comfort he and Elsie wanted. It had been Elsie who had suggested a land cruise in a coach. Always, she had wanted to do Scotland properly, and they'd never been there except once, when they'd spent two nights in Edinburgh for the tattoo. And they'd been abroad quite often enough, she said firmly. She was a little woman, bun-shaped and white, but she had always been firm even though, when Ernie had been still working, she had let him have his way over the annual holiday.

'This time,' she'd said, making a neat bundle of all the other travel brochures, 'it's bonnie Scotland for me and don't you try to argue against it!'

Ernie's reply had been submissive but rude. 'Just want to look up a Scotsman's kilt, that's all you want.'

She laughed. 'Get along with you!' She became practical. 'When we get back, see what's left, then...'

'Then what?'

'Alan could do with some help, couldn't he?' Alan was the only son, financially crippled possessor of a large mortgage. 'Help with the house, Ernie.'

He nodded, bird-like, compliant. 'Sure, sure, we'll see what we can do... when we get back. Have a good time first, eh?' And he'd added ghoulishly, because he had quite a lot of Whole Life Assurance with the company who did business with the London and South Coast Building Society, 'The boy'll be best off when we both kick the bucket, Elsie....'

* * *

Frank Harkness took Tour Eighteen on to the M1 with a sense of release, all ready to put his foot down. Looking right as he made to merge with the fast traffic, he caught sight of the two men, youngish men, in the off-side, single seats immediately behind him. Just a glimpse from the corner of his eye backed up the image received when they'd embarked. One of them was a sort of Dago-ish type, dark-faced with a drooping black moustache that ended somewhere beneath the chin on either side. Name... Kahn, that was it. Could be foreign, but spoke with a mid-Atlantic accent that gave nothing away positively. The man behind Kahn had arrived in a sweat at Victoria Coach Station, arrived only just in time. He was also young but of a different type, fresh-faced and sunny, with an Irish name—Kerrigan. Life on the road had taught Frank Harkness that there were, broadly, two kinds of Irishman; the long-faced, long-upper-lipped, dark and largely morose sort, and the happy, fair sort who laughed a lot and probably sang *The Rose of Tralee* in the bath. Mr Kerrigan seemed to be this latter sort, and above the noise of London's traffic Harkness had been aware of him talking and laughing and, apparently, trying to stir some life into those near him with whom, after all, he would have to spend the greater part of the next fourteen days. Being a touring car passenger, Harkness knew well enough, was a lottery. Often he had much sympathy for his passengers, and did what he could to shift the seating plan around after the first leg. This was not always easy: some people just wouldn't shift, wouldn't co-operate for the greater good.

Already, he'd come up against stiffness. Back at Victoria, two very old ladies had been placed immediately in front of two youngsters carrying transistor radios which they'd switched on, or one of them had, the moment they'd sat down. Harkness, casting an eye over his mixture, had smilingly approached a Mr and Mrs Hanborough in the front near-side pair of seats with a view to an exchange. They had both appeared to be on an age par with the very old ladies, and thus likely to be understanding, but Harkness's polite request had been coolly received, at least by Mrs Hanborough. The old man, tall and slim with a yellowish-white moustache and penetrating blue eyes, had cupped a hand around an ear and said, 'What's that?'

'I was wondering if you'd be willing to change your seat, sir.'

'Where to?'

Harkness indicated the seat with the transistors. 'Where those young folk are, sir.'

Hanborough levered himself round. 'Well . . .'

'Henry.'

The old man swung back, looking down at his wife, who was bundled in fur. 'Yes, my dear?'

'What is the man saying?'

'Oh, er... wants us to change our seats to further back. What d'you say—h'm?'

'Oh, no, I don't think so, Henry.' A withered hand clutched at neck fur, the face looked anxious, pinched. 'I believe these coaches *swing dreadfully*. We did book for the front, Henry.'

'Quite.' The blue eyes seemed to glare at Harkness frostily. 'My wife... *must* we move, driver?'

'No, no, no compulsion, sir, I only want everyone to be happy and comfortable, that's all—'

'Then we'll stay where we are,' the old man said with pointed finality and a flick of his hand, dismissing drivers. Frank Harkness, seeing no other likely changers as he made his way down the gangway nevertheless on a goodwill, getting-to-know-them mission, reflected that you couldn't blame the old couple really, but a bit of give-and-take on a tour went a long way. Already in his mental ear he heard the forthcoming complaints from the two old dears. Of course, it was within his province to ban the transistors on the road, but he didn't want to do that. Give-and-take again... with any luck, the old ladies were stone bloody deaf...

* * *

The Hanboroughs were in fact touring incognito: they hadn't much money, but they had position. Military peers, in Lady Hanborough's view, didn't go on coach trips, but Henry had been so set on seeing Scotland again that she had compromised. They would go, but not, please God, as Colonel Lord Hanborough and his lady wife. Thirty years before, when her husband had commanded a Lancer regiment, things had been so very different... thirty years of retirement had left little money for luxuries and they did need a holiday: their doctor had said so. Eastbourne, he had said, was a nice healthy place but one should get away from it once a year if possible. A change of air was a good tonic. He had very much approved the idea of Scotland, and the Colonel had made a nice little joke of the coach trip at the golf club. 'Can't be stand-offish and well, *insular*, in these democratic days.' He'd gone on to say, 'Not what we're used to, of course, but I'm sure it'll be fun.'

Speeding now along the M1 under the thrust of Frank Harkness's right foot, Lady Hanborough had a sudden, disturbing thought: they were both a little over eighty, and this could well be their last holiday before they died. And in the moment that this horrid thought came to her, something made her glance to her right, and, across her husband's unheeding hook nose, so very military and distinguished, she caught the most diabolical look from the man named, though she didn't know this, Kahn.

2

IN THE seat behind the driver as Tour Eighteen swept past the service area at Scratchwood, Kahn, darkly handsome, sat brooding, staring at the grey nylon back of Frank Harkness. It was a sort of four-square back, solid, with muscle rippling around the shoulder-blades when Harkness needed to turn the wheel. It was thick and strong despite a touch of surplus fat. Earlier, when embarking, Kahn had studied the face of Harkness: open, with a little pugnaciousness lurking for use when required. The face of a man of set opinions, a man who knew when he was right and when he was wrong, a man who would stand upon his rightness.

Kahn's gaze shifted, looking half left towards the old cow in the near-side front seat, the old cow whose eye he had caught a short way back and who had flinched like someone had given her bottom a pinch. Old, fragile lips working in a kind of chewing motion, with deep furrows running towards a small, tight mouth. Brown stains of old age on her hands when she removed her gloves. Not coach tour material, but Kahn happened to know this. And the old geezer: he was big boned and had had a good figure once. Now he was all skin and bone and looked as though he would fragment at a touch, disintegrate into dust like an Egyptian mummy given a shove in the gut two thousand years after death. Currently the old geezer was yacking at the missus—he had a loud haw-haw voice, and he was being informative, or reminiscent more accurately, about what had once been country before the arrival of the house builder and the motorway. Sixty years ago, the old geezer had hunted not far from Scratchwood: a far cry from the cups of tea, Pepsi, hamburgers, egg-and-chips, newspaper stalls, petrol pumps and lavatories of

Scratchwood today. Or Scratch Wood, as the old geezer kept on saying it, two words.

Thinking of lavatories, Kahn got to his feet. Tour Eighteen provided luxury, and luxury included a chemical toilet compartment at the rear. Kahn, taking his time, headed for it, down the fifteen-inch-wide gangway, putting on a pair of dark glasses. He looked at his fellow tourists. In one pair of seats was an elderly man with glasses much darker than Kahn's, and a white stick held upright between the knees like a safe stanchion—blind. Then why go on a sightseeing tour? Kahn grinned. The blind man's hands were gripping the handle of the stick, the knuckles standing out whitely. Beside him, a fairly obvious wife sat with one arm across her body, the elbow of the other arm resting on the back of the wrist, and her hand supporting her chin as she gazed out of the window at cars and concrete. They had the look of people who didn't speak much to each other. The wife was a lot younger than her husband, and not bad looking. Farther down, two youths, late-teenagers, were listening to a transistor. Pop music was being played just now, not loudly, but it was obviously going to ruin the tour for two old bags in black just ahead. One of them had ostentatious cottonwool visible, jamming her right earhole below a daft-looking hat. Behind the transistor listeners, a couple were all but performing the sex act, like they couldn't wait for the first overnight stop. They didn't even notice Kahn looking.

Kahn moved on, entered the toilet compartment. Here, he was right above the boot. Kahn thought about the boot; he was a meticulous man, and knew quite well that he hadn't forgotten anything, not the smallest detail, but nevertheless his mind roved, doing a mental check once again.

* * *

The Tannoy clicked on: there was a hum, then the voice of Harkness. 'We're coming up to the Toddington service area, ladies and gentlemen. We'll go in for elevenses. Twenty minutes, that's all, please, from when we stop. Next stop will be for lunch at Leicester Forest East. Thank you.' Click and off. Harkness flicked and moved left into the slow lane, then took the slip road into the service area, drew into the coach park, and stopped. He pulled himself out of the driving seat, stood up and stretched.

'Well, there we are, ladies and gents.' He wondered how long it would be before a degree of matiness would be acceptable, when the old dears would take being addressed as boys and girls—such a moment usually came, though it never failed to produce some stiff expressions. 'Twenty minutes, not a moment longer if you don't mind.' He smiled; his words had been authoritative and were as such intended, but the smile softened them: such a nice man, he wouldn't really leave without them all. Harkness looked down at the Hanboroughs. 'If you'd like to get down, sir, I'll give you a hand, you and the lady.'

Hanborough glanced at his wife. 'Ready, my dear?'

'I think I'll stay, Henry.'

'Oh, come! One has to stretch one's legs, we've a long journey—'

'I feel a little faint, Henry.'

'Then fresh air's what you need, Edie."

'No, no ...'

Harkness felt like saying, for God's sake make your minds up. But he didn't. Others, less patient, were already pushing past; the disembarkation was proceeding. 'So *rude*,' Lady, or Mrs, Hanborough was heard to say to her husband. In the end, they both stayed put, and the old man produced a small flask of whisky. Mark Graham and Jilly Ruff also stayed put, being too busy and liking the greater intimacy made possible by the exodus. Kahn and Kerrigan got down with the rest. Kerrigan sauntered off with his hands in his pockets, catching the eye of one Susan Larcombe—quite a bird, but in company with a possessive husband. Kerrigan, grinning, joined the queue for coffee.

Kahn went towards the telephone booths and dialled a Glasgow number. 'Toddington,' he said. 'Ten minutes behind schedule.' Then he rang off.

* * *

Tour Eighteen came off the motorway at Exit 25 for Toton in Nottingham. On came the Tannoy again: 'We pick up three more passengers at Toton, ladies and gents, just a quick halt if they're on time. Toton is a big British Rail diesel depot, but I reckon you're all past train spotting so we won't delay for that.'

His first little joke: the rear-view mirror showed a ripple of faint smiles, though half-left from his seat the Hanboroughs failed to register. The old man didn't look as though he'd ever train spotted. Harkness had, still remembered the thrill when he'd got his full set of Westerns, poor old engines now largely reduced to hauling freight, engines that raised pitying smiles from earnest seekers of Brush Fours, Deltics and what-have-you. He drove on for the pick-up point, which was to be just short of the Toton roundabout, so that Tour Eighteen could carry straight on round and back again for the motorway rather than penetrate deeper into Nottingham.

The three were waiting, nice and punctual. One man, two women—two sisters, spinster office workers, the Misses MacBean, exiles from their native land. The man, a young man, Rod Silver. Harkness got down, smiling in welcome, and headed for the boot, which he unlocked for the cases. The Misses MacBean both corrected him simultaneously when he pronounced their name Macbeen.

'Mac*bane*,' they said loudly.

'Sorry, ladies.' They had a case each, old-fashioned heavy suitcases with leather corners and two straps—like the man who wore braces as well as a belt in case one broke, Harkness thought. Mr Silver had three cases, one of them bloody heavy, which Mr Silver seemed particular about.

'Careful,' he said. 'Glass.'

'Glass?'

'Bottles. I take my own. It's cheaper!'

'In Scotland,' Harkness said, trying another joke, 'they may charge corkage.' He reflected that judging from the weight, Silver must have a heck of a thirst. He ushered his passengers aboard, pushed the door shut, settled the Misses MacBean into the seats right behind the American couple in a flurry of cardigans and paper carrier-bags, indicated Silver's seat right at the rear, then resumed his own seat. He started up, took the 31-seater, now full, round the roundabout and back to the northbound M1. The Misses MacBean, whose Scottish accents had caused the American daughter, Agnes MacFee, to catch their eye, fussily introduced themselves across the fifteen inches of gangway that separated Agnes from her parents, diagonally right from the MacBeans.

'We're from Scotland,' the elder MacBean said, 'so really we're going home.'

'Is that so?'

'Aye. Oh, we're looking forward to it tremendously!' Miss MacBean beamed through her spectacles. 'We've not been back for a year, you see.'

'A year?'

'We go back every year. This is the first time by coach, though, and we've a feeling it's going to be enormous fun, much more friendly than going alone by train. Oh, we're going to have a great time.' Miss MacBean beamed again. 'Are you American?'

Agnes MacFee said, 'Sure.'

'This is your first visit to—er—Britain?'

'Yes, I guess it is. But in a sense, we're coming home, me and my folks.' Agnes MacFee, who had a certain hard beauty, dark and high-cheek-boned, smiled and added, 'The name's MacFee. We're looking for ancestors, the clan home, you know? But all the information, I guess, says we kind of come from all over, know what I mean?'

Miss MacBean nodded cautiously: she did know, but preferred not to be too explicit. The clan MacFee, ancestrally, had all been tinkers. She knew of no chieftainly castle, no landed heritage.

* * *

Leaving the M1, leaving the M18, Harkness stopped again at a petrol station with refreshments attached, on the A1 north of Ferrybridge. He stopped for his passengers to get cups of tea; this time, they all got out and walked around a while. Kahn headed once again for the telephone, once again dialled the Glasgow number.

'Ferrybridge... on schedule at Toton, time made up. Silver aboard.' He paused. 'Anything to report?'

'Nothing. All's well, Lenny.'

'Good. I'll check in next from Darlington.'

Kahn rang off. Coming out of the booth, he bumped into Jilly Ruff and apologized briefly. He went to find a cup of tea and Jilly rang Horsham, feeling repentant about her huffy exit from home early that morning. 'Mum,' she said, and stopped. She added, 'It's Jilly.'

'Oh. I hope you're all right, love.'

'Course I am, Mum. Mark—'

'I don't want to hear about him, thank you. Jilly, just you watch it. Just you look after yourself, that's all. It's you that'll suffer, haven't I told you that often enough?' Mrs Ruff's voice was sharp with anxiety, with frustration, with a fairly vivid imagination. It only irritated Jilly, who said yes, well, quite enough, and now she had to go, goodbye. She rang off with an anger that didn't last and left her with fresh remorse, but even so she was damned if she was going to listen to lectures when all she'd wanted to do was to let Mum and Dad know she had got so far in safety. Jilly banged out of the telephone box with her cheeks flaming and went to the Ladies, preferring the genuine article to the facilities provided in the swaying coach.

* * *

Darlington and the overnight stop at an hotel on the outskirts: joy for Jilly and Mark. Separate rooms, of course, but night flitting was nicely unobserved. Although Lord Hanborough, paying a late visit to the lavatory, saw an eager Mark Graham, in pyjamas, sliding into a bedroom, it never occurred to him that the room was not Mark's own. That night Jilly was fulfilled: it was quite different in a real bedroom where you knew you wouldn't be disturbed. You could let yourself go with no reservations at all; it was a memorable night, with thirteen, or was it twelve, more to come. Jilly blossomed; after a while Mark fell asleep and she lay with his head cradled softly in her arms. She stroked his hair, ran a hand lightly down his naked back, loving the feel of warm skin.

Not such a good night for the Irishman, Kerrigan. One small sentence, uttered in the bar to Kahn earlier, expressed his total disappointment. 'Not one bloody bird on her own!'

Kahn drank Scotch, eyes hard. 'Forget it.'

'Christ, I can't!'

'You'll have to. There'll be a time for that, later.'

'Well—maybe.' Kerrigan toyed with his glass. 'Two of them are smashers—the one with the long dark hair, Jilly something, and the fair one . . . with a jealous husband.'

'Jilly Ruff and Susan Larcomb.'

Kerrigan grinned. 'Done your homework!'

'I hope—for your sake—you have.' There was a clear warning in Kahn's voice. 'And watch it: from now on out, no birds. Get yourself a sign saying 'Sold,' hang it on your flies.'

* * *

Like he always did, Frank Harkness had telephoned home to Mary and the kids. They all came on the line, every night when he was away, just as soon as he could get to a phone. First Mary, then Stevie, then little Frances.

Mary asked, as she always did on the first night, 'What are they like, Frank?'

'Much as usual. More younger ones maybe . . . some good lookers, but you don't have to worry!' He grinned into the mouthpiece. 'How's everything, eh?'

'All right. Except one burner's gone off on the cooker.'

'Ring 'em, did you?'

'It's only just gone off, Frank. I'll ring in the morning.'

'Okay, love.' He glanced at his watch, saw the American couple hovering, looking as though they wanted to use the phone. 'Put the children on, love.'

'All right.' There were kissing noises: Harkness made similar noises back. He smiled happily. His last remark, after Mary came back on the line and reminded him to ring the next night, was, 'If it's the last thing I ever do . . .'

In the morning he assembled his charges. The two old ladies in black, the objectors to transistors, couldn't be found at first. After a longish delay, which seemed to worry the dark-faced man, Kahn, beyond the normal, the old ladies were seen coming up the drive from the street: oblivious of time and schedules, they had gone for a walk to look at the shops. Harkness, who had once been a ship's steward and accustomed to remark that all passengers invariably labelled their brains Not Wanted On Voyage, was patiently chiding. Thus late, he took Tour Eighteen back on to the A1 for Edinburgh. He made up a little time and was not too far behind at Newcastle. With a deviation to take a quick look at Bamburgh Castle, he was scheduled for a lunch stop in Berwick and a 15.30 arrival in Edinburgh, where the second night would be spent. They would not leave Edinburgh until after lunch the following day. In Edinburgh, there was much to see. From Scotland's capital Tour Eighteen would cross the Forth road bridge into Fife, and on north for Perthshire, towards Inverness, staying the third night in Pitlochry on the A9.

* * *

The call from Edinburgh next day was taken in an office in Glasgow's dock area, an office, sparsely furnished, behind a garage. That call came from the telephone-prone Kahn and it was taken by a man in greasy overalls, a man named Rubery, who said little but listened much, nodding at intervals. When Kahn rang off, Rubery waited a moment then called a number in Milngavie, a little way down the Clyde.

Still brief, he said, 'We go in as planned. All okay.'
The voice rattled in his ear: 'On the sched?'
'Spot on. No troubles your ends?'
'None.'
'Right. Be with you in half an hour.' Rubery rang off, pushed himself back from the desk, swivelled his chair and got up. From outside came river sounds, the melancholy bray of sirens as outward-bound ships headed down the Clyde for the Tail o' the Bank, the Cumbraes, and the open sea beyond Ailsa Craig. Rubery crossed the office to a wall safe. Opening this, he brought out a 7.65 Walther PPK automatic which he pushed into the pocket of his overalls.

3

FRANK HARKNESS liked to give good value: Tour Eighteen went down from Edinburgh to North Queensferry for a close look at the rail bridge across the Forth. 'Grandad of the big cantilever bridges,' he said over the Tannoy. 'Takes three years to paint... 152-foot clearance for ships. During the war, some big stuff came and went underneath—*Hood*, *Repulse*, and some of the aircraft-carriers. The Germans used to try to block 'em in with bombs but they never succeeded in getting the bridge.'

There was a stir of nostalgia in old Hanborough's face—also, to a lesser degree since his war had been fought at a lower level, in that of Ernie Peach. From the younger element, blankness. It all meant nothing now. Halting the coach, Harkness pointed out a crummy, broken expanse of concrete jetty pushing in sad dereliction into the Firth of Forth. 'They say that was busy once, with boats from the Fleet. All gone now.' He lingered for a moment, looking, imagining back. He liked the Scottish tour because he had a feeling for history, and there was plenty of that in Scotland. A snatch of poetry came into his mind, something from way back, centuries before the Second World War: *Strike and drive the trembling rebels backwards o'er the stormy Forth; let them tell their pale Convention how they fared within the North....* He gave a small sigh, turned in his seat to look back along the body of the coach. The Misses MacBean were looking as they had looked ever since they had crossed the border; proud and swimmy-eyed. Harkness could understand the way they felt. Well, they would have plenty to get emotional about before they crossed the border again and left grandeur and the pipes behind them and returned to the workaday world of Nottingham. He got on the move again, along the narrow street with the tourist-orientated shops, beside the Firth, turned the coach, and headed back for the great road bridge whose almost delicate-looking span crossed the water like a grey rainbow, upstream from the now less fashionable heavy girders of the railway bridge.

On the bridge, he drove as slow as the regulations allowed and pointed out Rosyth Dockyard to the left. It was a sunny afternoon, and clear as a bell yet, though there was a hint, a feel, of approaching evening mist. Slanting down beside the carriageways from their towering supports the heavy cables appeared like something out of fairyland. On the slight upward rise as you approached the centre, there was a feeling almost of heavenward heading. From the passengers, even from Mark Graham and Jilly Ruff, there were sounds of awe. They seemed suspended, miles above blue water, with sun glinting on metal, and the river shimmering below. Cameras clicked. Only Kahn and Kerrigan in the front, Rod Silver in the back, seemed unmoved, taut.

Tour Eighteen came off the bridge, rolling on into the ancient Kingdom of Fife.

* * *

Along the A90 towards the city of Perth, pioneer of dry-cleaning: from there they would take the A9 for Dunkeld and Pitlochry. A full day, longish: the older passengers grew restless, wanting the motionless peace of the hotel. Lady Hanborough nodded off to sleep, head lolling against her husband and her mouth dribbling a little down his left sleeve. Back along the coach Ernie Peach was thinking of a pint of beer—Younger's Scotch Ale for preference. 'Get Younger Every Day.' He liked his evening pint—always had. The two old ladies in black suffered the sound of the transistor, their wrinkled mouths pursed; it was picking up Scottish sounds now, traditional airs, which they found not unpleasant. Jilly Ruff was now almost invisible beneath Mark Graham, and her eyes were closed, and her lips were parted: Mark was making good use of a roving hand, and of the cover of his jacket, removed and now doing duty as a rug, a rug in constant danger of slipping. With half an eye Rod Silver was watching. From behind them and to their right he couldn't in fact see much, but he could see a little and he had a good imagination. Farther up the coach the Misses MacBean talked together, pointing landmarks out to one another in loud, eager voices. The shades of evening were coming down now: as the coach, travelling fast, moved through Kinross into the Ochil Hills, the land became darkly purpled and shot with green, with the last of the day's sun slanting along the distant crests. They went through Perth. They were some five miles out of Perth on the A9 when Kahn got to his feet, moved into the gangway alongside Kerrigan, glanced down the coach and caught the eye of Rod Silver. Fractionally, Silver nodded.

Kahn closed in on Frank Harkness, bent to speak to him.

'Next turn right, signposted Stanley, Murthly and Caputh. Take it, all right?'

Harkness turned his head in surprise. The coach swerved, came back: Harkness had seen the small round hole, the muzzle of Kahn's automatic. 'What the bloody hell!' He slowed.

'*Keep going.* Do just as I tell you and you won't get hurt. Nor will anybody else. Be sensible.'

Harkness swallowed. He looked in his mirror. Kerrigan was on his feet, holding on to the back of his seat, staring down the coach. At the back, Silver was standing too. Harkness swallowed again, felt ice along his spine. He thought fast. He didn't want trouble, and, though he was obviously going to get it, it might be wiser to delay it as long as possible. Hoarsely he asked, 'Where are we going, then?'

'You'll see soon enough. Do as I say, that's all you have to do.' The gun moved towards him. 'Next turn right. After that, I'll tell you.'

Harkness did as he was told. His heart thumped and thudded. Tour Eighteen flicked right, took the turn for Caputh. Harkness glanced up at Kahn: there was a gleam in the dark eyes; the down-swept thin black moustache looked devilish. Another look in the mirror: some of the faces seemed puzzled at seeing Kahn and Kerrigan on their feet, but none of the passengers had as yet seen the gun or guessed what was happening, though the Misses MacBean were looking more puzzled than the rest. Even old Hanborough, close as he was to Harkness, hadn't ticked over. A couple of miles beyond Stanley, Harkness got his next route order—right, on to a mere single-track road, or not much more. The coach lurched over a poor surface, windows swept by branches.

'Look,' Harkness said desperately, 'We—'.

'Shut up and do as you're told.'

Harkness shrugged and drove on. Behind him, there was tension now, bewilderment: he could see that in his rear-view mirror. They were looking round, half rising in their seats, yacking at each other, asking what was up. One of the younger men, Larcombe, the one with the birdie wife, started to walk up along the gangway, Adam's apple agitating in a long neck. Harkness heard Kerrigan's voice: 'Sit down, you! Sit down *all* of you.'

Someone, Harkness didn't know who, screamed. Hanborough's eyes widened. He put a protective arm round his wife and called sharply to Frank Harkness.

'I say there—driver! This man's pointing a gun—'

Kerrigan moved a little: gun steady in his right hand, he brought his left arm across his body and landed a vicious back-swipe on Hanborough's face. The old man gave a gasp, and blood ran from his nose and from a split lip. 'Shut up, you old fool!' Kerrigan snapped. He raised his voice. 'Keep in your seats, all of you. The first one to try anything at all, gets the first bullet. Keep quite still, keep quite quiet, and nothing'll happen to you.'

They cringed away from his voice, fearful, dumbfounded. The two French women began a rapid, monotonous gibber, round the side of their seats. In the back, Silver now had his gun visible. The coach was commanded, under full control and the expressions of the three men showed their determination clearly. Time dragged. The coach moved on towards the Highlands above Strathmore, keeping so far as possible to the by-roads. Frank Harkness, bewildered, scared, anxious for his passengers and for what Mary would be thinking when he failed to ring from Pitlochry, obeyed the given route orders but soon lost his sense of direction and whereabouts. He felt they were going north and that was all. The country grew harsher as it grew darker—harsher, more jagged, with the road running below rearing crests, dead isolated, dead lonely. It grew colder, too.

* * *

'If only we'd never come!' Elsie Peach was shaking and her face was white. She kept clutching her husband's arm and pulling at a string of Woolworth's pearls. 'Oh, Ernie, what are we going to do, what's going to happen to us?'

He said half-heartedly, 'Just don't worry, nothing we can do just now, is there?'

'If only we'd never come....'

He patted her arm, as scared as she. 'There, there, we'll come through, they can't want anything of *us*, can they now?'

In front, old Hanborough was staring bleakly at Kerrigan and his gun. Just staring, from that blood-smeared face. In the old days he could stare anybody out, from private soldier to general—he was Lord Hanborough, an aristocrat with private means, now eroded. Higher rank hadn't abashed him. But this dreadful man, this outsider, just met his stare and grinned, and he found that disconcerting though he didn't, he hoped, show it. As he stared, he fumed and rumbled impotently. Had he been a younger man... but perhaps a time would come. They couldn't keep up this nightmare ride for ever. In the meantime there was Edie—always, he prayed, there would be Edie. His arm was around her, comforting her. Through her clothing he could feel the pounding of her heart. She wasn't speaking now, though she'd woken up; she was just staring ahead through the windscreen, petrified by the world's brutality, by the proximity of the sort of person of whom she had no experience whatever.

Behind the Hanboroughs, right down the coach, the transistor was now switched off. The two youths, Ben Hurst and Peter Brewster from Uxbridge, didn't want to miss out on anything that was said. They had a sort of ready look, as though they had it in mind eventually, when the time was right, to be heroes. In front of them, the two old ladies in black had a withdrawn air, as though they were trying to pretend nothing was happening. They looked out of their window, and at each other, with wide eyes and working mouths, and they held hands tightly, but they made no sound, hoping, perhaps, that whatever it was that was nasty would go away if not provoked. Behind again, Jilly Ruff was also wide-eyed, sitting stiffly upright, dead scared but trusting Mark to get her out with a whole skin. She thought a lot about Mum and Dad, with a very sinking heart. *They*'d been scared about a fate worse than death, but if they could see her now, their worries might be different and more pointed.

* * *

Kahn spoke. 'Not far now. Watch out for a red Cortina, parked left.'

Harkness nodded. He looked out into his headlamp beams: they whitened firs, or maybe they were pines—thick forest, anyway, dark beyond the lights, very dark and close-set. The air coming through his driving window was colder than before, with a hint of frost to come. Another couple of miles and he picked up the car.

Looking ahead now, Kahn said, 'Slow. Stop behind it.' He swung round. 'Nobody moves, all right?'

Nobody moved. The coach came to a stop just behind the Cortina.

'Leave the engine running.'

There was a comparative silence now, broken by footsteps approaching the doors—the driver's, the passengers'. A face looked in at Harkness and another gun was pointed at him. Two men mounted the steps of the passenger door, stood, also with guns, looking down the gangway. One of them lifted an eyebrow at Kahn. 'No trouble, then?'

'No trouble.'

The man nodded. 'Fine! We'll get on, shall we?' He looked down at Harkness. 'Tummel Bank Hotel, right?'

Harkness stared. 'What about it?'

'Where you were booked in?'

Dully, Harkness nodded. They *knew*—no point in a denial. He said, 'Yes, that's right.'

'You'll have gathered you won't be going there.' Just for a split second, the man grinned. It didn't improve his face. 'Ring your wife every night, don't you, on tour?'

'Me?' Harkness thought he saw a possible way. 'No, I—'

'Don't waste your breath—or my time. You've been researched, Driver Harkness. So has a lot of things. You're going to ring your wife again tonight. Sparrow will take the coach.' The man leaned across Harkness, called to the man in the night, the man at the driving window. 'Hop up, Sparrow. You,' he added to Harkness, 'out this way, and take it easy, very, very easy.'

Harkness came out from behind the wheel. Sparrow climbed in. Ahead of the other man's gun, Harkness got down from the passenger door on to springy turf, into the cold air, into yet another gun. He was told to get into the Cortina, where sat Rubery from Glasgow behind the wheel. As he got in, the coach moved. It pulled out past the Cortina, and Harkness, looking up, saw the scared faces of his passengers. The big vehicle went ahead a little way, then turned off left, seemingly right into the forest, and vanished from sight. When the Cortina moved, Harkness, looking left, saw the tail-lights of the coach moving along a clear, narrow path, like a ride, making deep into the cover of the trees, lurching, moving slow. The Cortina went on ahead with Frank Harkness in the back, between two guns. Rubery drove fast. On either side, the deep forest spread, silent, lonely, utterly deserted like the road. After five miles they reached a main road, and turned right. Another ten miles or so, ten miles of no speaking from the car's occupants, they stopped at an RAC telephone kiosk. The two men in the back got out with Harkness. One of them used his key: inside, Harkness felt crowded, desperate, found that he was sweating like a pig in spite of the cold night air.

The man who had done the speaking in the coach, took charge. 'You ring your wife,' he said. His gun pressed into Harkness, as did the other man's. 'You convince. You don't sound rattled.'

'How can I—'

'Pull yourself together. You're breathless. Control it. If you can't control it one hundred per cent, say you've been running. You've broken down—the coach has, but you're all right. You broke down on the road running through Buchanty and Chapelhill... you took a wrong turn in Perth, and were heading back for the A9, north from Gilmerton. Here.' The man opened up a Shell Road Atlas, and stubbed at it with a forefinger. 'Gilmerten—Foulford Inn —Buchanty. You're calling her from Buchanty. Got it?'

'Yes—'

'Put it across, Harkness. No mistakes, no hesitations. We don't mind killing you.' He stared into Harkness's eyes. 'There's something else. We know your home address, Harkness. There'll be a watch kept. I think you understand ... don't you?'

Harkness licked at dry lips and stared back. There was a terrible feeling in his guts, and his hands shook, but the thought of Mary and the children in possible danger had a concentrating effect. He took up the receiver, got the exchange, asked for his home number. The wait was not long. His heart pounded when Mary answered, but he held steady because he knew he had to, that his family depended on it. He managed: he convinced Mary. If he left her worried as to how he was to pass the night, she was no more worried than he. After this, he was told to call the Tummel Bank Hotel in Pitlochry, and he did this satisfactorily too, giving the same story. Then back to the car.

* * *

The coach was well hidden. It had been driven a long way up the ride from the road and had turned left into deep forest, virtually wedged between trees in a small clearing. The passengers were still inside and the coach was in semi-darkness, lit only by one interior light and occasionally the beam of a torch held by Kahn who was on guard up front, with Silver still at the back. Harkness was pushed aboard and reports were made to Kahn, who seemed happy. It was, to

Harkness, eerie, for his car—as, in busman's talk, he thought of the coach—to be so full and yet so silent, as though all life had gone from it. The passengers were dazed now: so many of them were too old to take this sort of caper, to take being hijacked. Now and again the silence was broken by sobs, and at one point the MacFees began yattering in loud tones about the American Embassy in Grosvenor Square, and what the ambassador would be doing on their behalf. Kahn stopped the name-dropping by aiming his gun at MacFee's head. Harkness, feeling a big weight of responsibility towards all these people, made an effort to obtain information. He had tried this in the Cortina, but had been silenced. Now, he appealed to Kahn, the obvious leader.

'What are you trying to do?' he asked.

Kahn said, 'Shut up, can't you,' and beamed his torch down the coach, lighting up Silver. 'Okay, Rod. Kerrigan's coming down now.' He nodded at Kerrigan, who moved towards the rear, holding his gun ready. At the back, he turned to watch the passengers, and Silver pushed past him towards the exit door. Kahn handed him the keys from the ignition. Silver jumped down. They saw his torch moving around the coach towards the rear. One of the men from the Cortina, Rubery from Glasgow, got into the coach, and stood by Kahn, looking dangerous. Harkness heard the boot being opened up and a good deal of racket as things were brought out. The next time he saw Silver, Silver was dressed in overalls, with gauntlet gloves, wellingtons and a kind of visored helmet, and was bearing a battery-operated, paint-spraying outfit. One of the other men carried an axe and a saw. Harkness caught on: they were to be camouflaged. The operation started at once. The axeman cleared away the touching branches, giving Silver room to work with his cans of cellulose. He worked fast, in torchlight, expertly: Silver was a craftsman. Nevertheless, it would be a long job, Harkness thought. And a long job it was, continuing through the night. In the course of that night, there was another job to be done. That job, in its initial development, woke Harkness, who had dropped into an uneasy, shallow sleep behind his wheel. He heard a succession of sounds: an oath, a sharp cry, a gunshot that sounded, in the closed coach, like heavy artillery at arm's length, then a scream from a woman. Harkness looked along the coach. Mrs Larcombe, the birdie wife, was standing with her mouth wide open and her hands clenched to the sides of her head, that head of superb blonde hair—standing and screaming, looking down at her husband who was lying full length in the gangway beside the door of the toilet compartment. Kerrigan, his eyes faintly scared in the light of Kahn's torch, was staring down and Larcombe was not moving. A pool of blood slowly gathered beside his body, moved sluggishly out towards Ernie and Elsie Peach.

Kerrigan said, almost in apology, 'He went to the toilet... tried to get my gun.'

'Dead?' This was Kahn—crisp, cool.

'I... don't know, Lenny.'

'Christ! Find out, will you?'

Kerrigan bent and felt, struggling to turn Larcombe over. After a while he looked up. 'Dead,' he said.

Kahn swept his torch over the living, and spoke harshly. 'You've all had a warning now. Take note of it. We're not here for peanuts.'

As they got the body out of the coach, dragging it past Susan Larcombe, she fainted. Over the next hour the rest of them listened to the sounds as a makeshift grave was hacked out between the trees. Sudden and terrible change had come: now they all knew they were in the hands of killers.

4

DAWN, stealing slow but crisp through the forest, showed the completed re-spray. Tour Eighteen was now all-over maroon, no trace left of its original blue and gold. The number plates had been changed and, importantly to Kahn no doubt, the job had been done cleanly; no paint spillage anywhere, not a telltale drop on ground or trees. When Harkness was brought out to take a look— for Silver was proud of his craftsmanship—he noticed this clean work with grudging admiration and decided that the ground had probably been sheeted with canvas strips. He asked, looking at the nice fresh cellulose, 'Does this mean we move out?'

'When we're good and ready,' Kahn said, 'and that won't be before tomorrow. First, we have to paint in the coach's life story, right?'

Harkness nodded; this he understood. South of England Motor Services Limited had gone so the coach had to have an owner with an address, and first the maroon coating had to harden enough to take it and look good. He asked, 'what are you going to put on, then?'

Kahn said, 'Boscombe's Coach Hire, East Ham. We don't need the cover for too long—you'll see. Just remember who you belong to when you drive off, that's all.'

So he was to carry on with the driving: well, there might be some hope in that, perhaps, though it was unlikely they would be taking chances. Harkness didn't want a bullet like Larcombe, yet he had a responsibility. His mind raced as he was ordered back into the coach to bring out the chemical toilet-bucket for emptying. Under guard, he penetrated into the forest with the bucket, which he emptied absently: sudden stops, he thought—something up with the engine— something might turn up. But at the back of every thought was the spectre of Larcombe and a dread of what might happen to Mary and the children. After he had got back in, Rubery and one of the other men went off in the Cortina for an undisclosed destination and Silver, now out of his overalls, brought one of his cases out of the boot and produced breakfast; dry bread, one slice each; some energy tablets, one of glucose, one of malted milk; plus a mouthful of water from bottles.

Towards the back, a radio was switched on—softly, but Kahn heard it and went down the gangway. 'Give,' he said, and took the transistor from Ben Hurst. He swung round on the others. 'All radios out. Don't try hiding any. I might get rough.'

Kahn and Silver collected them in, and Silver took them to the boot. Kahn brought out a set of his own and said with a grin, 'May as well listen to the news on mine.'

It was early for the news. They listened to pop, and Hanborough began to shake with nerves exacerbated by the strident noise, worse because otherwise the coach was quiet. 'Must we have that?' he demanded. 'Isn't it bad enough—'

Kahn made a swipe in his direction and he flinched away, champing angrily. Kahn, waiting for the news, looking weary after a whole night on guard duty, made another announcement: 'Shaving will now take place. It'll take place every morning. You look too scruffy to be honest, fare-paying coach passengers, gentlemen.' He brought an electric shaver from his pocket, battery operated. After using it himself he passed it round—Hanborough first. Harkness was last, and felt better for ridding himself of his stubble. Soon, the early news, dismal as ever, but a relief from the fast, non-stop rat-a-tat-tat from the French women that had accompanied the shaver's burr; Belfast, strikes, oil difficulties, cost-of-living, a big pile-up on the M1 in fog. Mary used to say, why bother to depress yourself? No word of a missing coach, of thirty-one passengers and a driver at the mercy of murderers. Harkness, swivelling in his seat, looked back along the coach, looked at the white, tired faces, at the hopeless expressions of people existing in fear of death. They all knew now what it must be like for the hostages in a hijacked aircraft—that was what *they* were, hostages.

Why? What were these men after? There had been no clue yet, no hint at all. And what were any of them worth to a hijacker? But of course that always applied: they were valuable just as lives—maybe! The world was growing sick and tired of hijacks. The authorities might be in no mood to give in to demands just to save the lives of a collection of senior citizens with a sprinkling of youth....

But those were not the lines to think along: you had to cling to hope, right up to the end, or you were already half done for.

Suddenly, coming out of the daze he had dropped into, Hanborough spoke up. 'Look here. I don't know what you're doing, but you'll never get away with—with keeping us here like this. I can't speak for the others, but it's certainly going to be remarked upon if I'm missing for long. Do you know who I am?'

He had addressed Kahn. Kahn lifted an eyebrow. 'Don't tell me, let me guess.' He screwed up his eyes as if in thought. 'No. It's no use. You'll have to end the suspense.'

'I'm a retired army officer, Lancers, and I'm a peer of the realm—Lord Hanborough.'

'No!'

'I assure you—'

Kahn waved a hand. 'Forget it, grandad, just forget it. It doesn't signify. It really doesn't. I knew it already, anyhow.'

Hanborough was speechless.

* * *

When Susan Larcombe had fainted, Elsie Peach had asked to be allowed to sit with her. This had been granted, and she was still with the girl. Susan had come round after a few minutes and had sat in a state of shock, not crying, not speaking. Elsie Peach had made her sniff some smelling-salts, which had caused her to choke a little and had brought the only tears to her eyes. She was stiff with grief, with suffering; Elsie could get nothing out of her, do nothing with her. She just sat through what was left of the night, and through the early morning, with one arm jerking like a marionette's. It was only after Hanborough's little effort that Elsie began to get an inkling. Susan seemed to have heard Hanborough, and her lips had parted though she hadn't uttered—but she seemed to be trying to. She stared rather wildly at Elsie, and wagged her head from side to side, and shook all through her slim body, staring still, and somehow pleading. It was then that Elsie realized, and felt a rush of blood to her head, a wave of sheer anger that wouldn't allow her to do anything other than call out to Kahn.

'You beasts!' she said in a high voice. 'You brutes, she can't speak! The shock, don't you see... it's made her dumb!' Then, as her husband came dangerously across to her, risking bullets, she put her head in her hands and wept.

* * *

Rubery and his companion came back just after noon, after there had been another issue of iron rations. The first sight of the two men raised wild hopes and an outburst of cheering, for they came back unrecognizable, dressed as police officers, in a police car complete with flashing blue lamp which pulled into the clearing behind the coach. When they were recognized and Rubery gave a friendly wave to Kahn, the whole situation worsened for the hostages. Jilly Ruff started a low sort of keening, and Kerrigan came along and slapped her silent, hard, prodding his gun at Mark Graham. Rubery made a report to Kahn.

'All okay.'

'Jacko's all set, is he?'

Rubery nodded. 'Sure thing.' He tilted his cop cap to the back of his head. 'First contact, 21.00 hours tonight.'

'Fine!' Kahn smiled. They were all listening hard, hanging on the passing words, and this he seemed to relish. He waved his gun-hand. 'That's all you're going to know,' he said. After this, the watch was at last handed over. The two men who had entered the coach from the Cortina the night before, plus Rubery, took over. Kahn, Kerrigan and Silver bunked down on three sets of seats and slept, having moved the occupants out to double-bank other seats. Jilly Ruff and Mark, the two old ladies in black, and the Misses MacBean were spread throughout the rest of the coach, uncomfortably. One of the MacBean women sat with Ernie Peach while his wife remained trying to comfort Susan Larcombe. The other MacBean, the elder, found herself adjacent to the MacFee parents, the ancestor seekers, now foiled in their search. To these she talked in a rapid, nervous voice, saying she was fairly sure of their whereabouts—Braemar, she said, not so far from Balmoral. She hadn't had an opportunity to date of discussing this with anyone but her sister—in the circumstances of their current existence, it was virtually impossible for the passengers to intercommunicate—but the somewhat useless imparting of her calculations seemed to bring her a strange comfort, as though they must be all right if they were close to the Queen.

* * *

That night Silver, back in overalls, got to work again painting in the details of ownership on the rear of the coach working as cleanly as before, leaving no evidence behind. Tonight there were no phone calls: Harkness, worrying about Mary, wondered why. Presumably, if the need to lull was now past, things were about to happen: that could tie up with Rubery's statement earlier—first contact 21.00 hours. But 21.00 hours came and went and no contact was made. They remained in the forest, hemmed in by the trees, hemmed in by silence, held suspended in their isolation. At intervals throughout the day, Rubery had listened to Kahn's transistor radio, and he listened again with Kahn at 21.30 hours. The BBC News, once again, was much as before. They listened again at 23.15: Kahn seemed to be expecting something positive now, though there was no disappointment, no apparent anxiety, when the something failed to materialize. Once more the night was passed uncomfortably under the guarding guns, but there was no more killing. After Larcombe, no-one was taking chances: a lesson had been learned. The passengers slept fitfully, eased cramped limbs, muttered in sleep. The women's faces were tear-stained. The eyes of the wakeful followed every movement of their warders as, throughout the long night, they changed the watches in the dim glow from the one interior light that was still burning. Harkness, his body gripped by a terrible restlessness, looked down along the ranks of seats from his place behind the wheel. He thought about Hanborough—a peer, and a soldier. The obvious, the natural leader? Once, maybe; not now. He was too old, both in mind and body. You could see from his face, his staring, red-rimmed eyes, that this situation was way beyond him. Who, then, was going to be the one to lead? No-one stood out; with the possible exception of the two with the radios, none of the men looked like men of action—and Larcombe, the one who had tried, the one who might have led, had died. Harkness, the driver, the captain of the ship, felt that it was he himself to whom the passengers must naturally look for help. But hunched behind his motionless wheel, he was as helpless as the rest of them. All he could usefully do, perhaps, would be to maintain an outward confidence, a determined cheerfulness in the face of trouble.

At last he slept, his body falling across the wheel. He was woken by the early news from Kahn's transistor radio. The disembodied voice, precise, emotionless, calm, came to the listening passengers on a curious note of intimacy, invading the coach to tell them of their fate, speaking to them and about them. 'A coach belonging to South of England Motor Services of Hounslow has been reported missing on a tour of Scotland. There has been no contact with this coach, which is carrying thirty-one passengers, mostly from London and the south, since Monday evening when it was believed to be in the vicinity of Buchanty in Perthshire. All Scottish police forces have been alerted following receipt of an anonymous telephone call at the Home Office at nine o'clock last night. This telephone call indicated that the coach and its passengers had been hijacked and would not be handed back until certain long-term prisoners were released from Pentonville Prison, delivered to a former RAF airfield in East Anglia, where an aircraft would be in readiness, and their safe arrival at an undisclosed destination confirmed. The names of the prisoners concerned have not been released by the Home Office, but it is thought likely that George Cunliffe, Harold Delabier and Frederick Massey, all serving thirty-year sentences for their part in the Bucksdown Heath spy case, may be involved.'

'Got it in one, the clever bastards,' Kahn said, switching off his radio. He looked down the gangway, grinning. 'So now you know, ladies and gentlemen.'

Old Hanborough was bristling. 'Damn traitors!' he said loudly. 'Surely you don't think the authorities are likely to let them go, do you?'

'If they don't,' Kahn said, fondling his automatic, 'you've got just a few more days to live. That goes for all of you, all right? So you'd better start praying that the Home Office sees sense. They didn't say it on the radio, but there's a deadline: 02.00 hours, Monday.' He grinned again, parting with more information. 'That's when you may be called upon to depart this life... with a nice, big bang.'

* * *

They had been expecting something like this: it hadn't been hard to work out. But the confirmation carried its own shock, made worse by the setting of the time-limit: it was not nice to know when you might die. You could start counting the hours now. Harkness found himself doing just that, his head bursting with thoughts of home, of what Mary would now be going through. He heard desperate sobs, looked round and saw the girl Jilly Ruff on her feet, swaying, face held in tight-pressed hands. From the back of the coach Kerrigan came forward, swung her round roughly, and gave her a couple of back-handers like Kahn had given Hanborough right at the start. When she cried more, Kerrigan shook her like a rat, her head lolling backwards and forwards. No-one went to her assistance, not even Mark Graham, who just sat and stared sickly. The fate of Larcombe had unmanned them all, and they were too preoccupied with the looming fact of mass death. Kerrigan let go of Jilly Ruff, then pushed her down into her seat.

'Just shut it,' he said. 'You're upsetting everybody.'

'What about my mum and dad?'

'What about them? Not here, are they?'

'No.' Jilly's whole body shook, her voice trembled in unison with it. 'What are they going to do? They never wanted me to come, they didn't...'

'That's too bad. Should have listened to them, shouldn't you?' Kerrigan, moistening his lips, looked down at her. He was stripping her bare, seeing small tight breasts, curves and dark places, but she didn't notice. He would have liked to make her notice him. Very much he wanted her body: it was a superb one. Well, maybe he would, before 02.00 hours on Monday—Kahn permitting, of course. Kahn might not permit; Kahn liked minds kept on the job till it was over. Kerrigan swung away, back to his station in the rear, watching, ready with his gun, the gun that he fondled as avidly as he would fondle a woman's body. Whistling softly to himself... thinking of the other good-looker, Larcombe's wife—Larcombe's widow—Susan. He wondered what it would be like with a girl who'd gone dumb. The experience might bring back her voice... Kerrigan grinned at the thought. He found something erotic in it: he'd heard of women who got an added thrill from having it off with one-legged men... no accounting for sexual tastes. Maybe before Monday, he would make a chance for himself with them both, out of the sight of Kahn. Kerrigan's mind busied itself with thinking up ways and means.

* * *

'We move,' Kahn announced. He announced this ten minutes after the early news broadcast. Harkness looked up. Once on the move, a time might come... but Kahn's next words dashed this frail hope. Kahn said, 'We move, and you'll be in the driving seat, Harkness, but you won't be driving long. Not once we hit the road—you'll see.'

Harkness asked, 'Why do we move? Isn't it better—from *your* point of view—if we stay put?'

Kahn shook his head. 'Poor thinking. There'll be a hunt on now, won't there? This is the sort of place they'll have in mind, right?'

'Yes, I s'pose so.'

'Where will they never think we'll be? I'll tell you—on the road! So we move, Harkness. Get ready to back her out. When you enter the track for the road, right hand down and then take her out front first.' He raised his voice to the passengers. 'All of you, listen hard. When we're—'

'You can't get away with it,' MacFee broke in loudly. 'Look, just as soon as the American Embassy got to hear—'

'Shut up.' Kahn moved along the gangway, pointing his gun. When he reached MacFee he took him by the hair, yanked him upright, then slammed a fist into his stomach. MacFee crumpled. The wife and daughter screamed. Kahn sauntered back up the gangway and turned to address the passengers again. 'Like I was saying. When we're on the road, you act like any other tourists on a nice, happy tour. You look relaxed, you look interested, you don't try anything funny like attracting attention or shouting messages. The windows, by the way, stay shut. Me and Kerringan'll be behind the driver, Silver at the back. We'll all be watching. I reckon you know the score by now.' He nodded at Harkness. 'Okay, take her out. Wait a moment, though, just a tick.'

Kahn got down. Harkness saw him walk around the coach, studying ground and trees with minute care, making one last final check, apparently, that Silver's work really had been dead clean and had left no traces of paint. Satisfied, Kahn climbed back in and nodded again at Harkness. Harkness switched on the ignition and started the engine. It fired at the third twist of the key. Khan leaned over. 'How's the fuel?'

'Half a tank.'

'How far—if we need it?'

Harkness stared. 'If we need it?'

'You'll see. Just answer the question. How far have we?'

'Hundred and fifty miles.'

'Fine. Where we're going, there'll be more in reserve—no worries, just checking!' Kahn grinned, stood in the front while Harkness backed out thirty-six feet of coach a little over eight feet wide, and headed for the road. Harkness had half a mind to step on the gas, for what good it might do, and belt regardless, heading for the first sign of the law; but the thought, which was a stupid one anyway, was still-born. Rubery in his cop uniform and cop car, was going down the track ahead of the coach. 'Left at the end,' Kahn said. 'And take it slow. You'll see a breakdown outfit pulled into the side. Stop behind it.'

Wonderingly, Harkness drove down the track, between the dark green of the conifers, thick-set, high: overhead, a clear blue sky, another beautiful day for Tour Eighteen's passengers, Scotland at its wonderful best. Reaching the road Harkness turned left, saw the breakdown vehicle, and stopped close behind it, following Kahn's instructions. Kahn jumped down, and was approached by the driver of the breakdown lorry. A tow was passed; Harkness nudged his gear-lever into neutral. The towing vehicle started up. Preceded by Rubery, they got moving again, and Harkness could only marvel at Kahn's brazen effrontery, at his strategy. It was a risk, but obviously a lesser one than being caught in the clearing before time. Who was going to query a coach under tow, a coach that was not blue and gold but maroon and did not belong to South of England Motor Services—a coach with fresh number plates, and preceded by all the glory of a police patrol car with flashing blue light?

5

CRUELLY, the repercussions were felt in a number of homes in London and the south. Local police stations took the telephone calls and the personal visits from anxious sons and daughters and other relatives. In Peckham, Mary Harkness had been questioned by officers of the Special Branch, led by a man named Daintree. She had not been able to help beyond giving them details of Frank's last telephone call from Scotland, which she said, when pressed, had sounded genuine.

'Definitely him?'
'Oh, yes...'
'Under threat?'
'I—I don't know.'
'How did he sound?'

She hesitated. 'Well—breathless. He said he'd been running—I told you.' Her voice was little more than a whisper. 'I suppose it could have been done under threat, but I don't know... Frank's always been conscientious. He loves his work, takes a pride in making his passengers happy. He'd have been thinking of them. He wouldn't ever do anything dishonest.'

Daintree said, 'That, we never thought. We've checked his record with the bus company. It's a good one.'

Mary Harkness was left with her worries. In Horsham, Jilly Ruff's parents were sick with anxiety, regretting not having parted on happier terms. For all concerned it was an utterly helpless feeling. Matters were entirely beyond them, out of their hands as the long wait for news began, as the questions remained unanswered: would the authorities accede to the terrorists' demands, or would thirty-two people be sacrificed? Were the police pulling out all the stops in their attempt to find the coach before the Monday deadline?

And if they did find the coach, what then?

* * *

In Whitehall, the echo of this last question: 'If it's found —then what?'

A shrugging of shoulders: it wouldn't be the first time hijackers had killed—they all had that much in mind. It was a high-level conference of the brass at the Home Office, involving the Commissioner of Metropolitan Police, Daintree from the Special Branch and other top men from the Home Office itself and from the Cabinet Office. The September sun slanted through big windows, gleaming along the polish of mahogany that seemed at variance with functional steel filing-cabinets. The silent, inexorable sweep of the second hand of an electric wall clock provided an unnecessary reminder of time passing. The deadline was 02.00 on Monday: right now, it was 11.32 on the Wednesday.

There was, as ever with hijacks, the cleft-stick situation. The man from the Home Office, big, wide-shouldered, pugnacious, removed heavy spectacles and rubbed at his eyes: the sun, catching him as he leaned forward, showed the whiteness of his face and the lines of strain running from darkly-shadowed eyes. He said, 'For my money, they're as good as dead. We all know how it goes, don't we? The moment anyone moves in...' He threw up his arms. 'Fanatics are virtually uncopeable with. And this time...'

'The bogey of International Communism?' This was Frazer-Petrie from the Cabinet Office. His remark came out with a laugh that fell upon stony ground and was met with a cold stare from the Commissioner. The involvement of Cunliffe, Delabier and Massey pointed the way only too clearly and the signs said Moscow: Bucksdown Heath was too fresh in everyone's memory. Bucksdown Heath had been big, the biggest spy scandal in years that had all but blown the major part of NATO's radar screen against attack. Cunliffe, Delabier and Massey had been arrested only just in time, before they had parted with the latest secrets. As it was, they had parted with a good deal. The rest was still in their heads and had to remain there. When the anonymous message had reached the Home Office the night before, the Prime Minister had been contacted immediately, called from a big dinner in the City. He had gone back to that dinner-table with a long face and absent eyes and manner, and he'd soon made his excuses and left for Downing Street. But in the meantime his answer had gone uncompromisingly to the concerned quarters: there would be no handing over of prisoners from Pentonville, come what may. This morning at the Home Office, Frazer-Petrie had told the brass there had been no overnight change of heart on the part of the Prime Minister.

'Understandable,' had been the Commissioner's comment. 'Bucksdown Heath apart, we can't open the floodgates. This time we have to win, just have to.'

'What d'you propose?' This was the Home Office man.

The Commissioner waved a hand towards the Special Branch. Commander Daintree took over. 'Saturation search in Scotland, sir. The area around Buchanty has already been covered, result nil. We believe that could have been a blind—in fact we're certain. But we're not all that short of time. I believe we have ... reasonable hopes.'

That was when the question had been asked. 'If it's found —then what?' It was largely rhetorical, and the shrugged shoulders were answer enough. But after the Home Office man had commented upon fanatics, Daintree had gone on with certain of his proposals. If the coach should be found, it would not be attacked, merely shadowed—at any rate, in the first instance. Attack might have to come, but when it did, it would be in strength and it would be fast. Meanwhile there were the other places; until the organization behind the hijackers indicated which airfield was to be used for the hand-over, all one-time airfields in East Anglia, and elsewhere too as a precaution, would be under hidden surveillance. Also in the meantime, Daintree said, flourishing a nominal list of the passengers aboard Tour Eighteen, the backgrounds of all aboard would be under investigation, a process that had already started. None of the names, Daintree said, were known either to Security or to Scotland Yard's various Criminal Record Office indexes, but the given names might not be the real ones. At the same time there would be intensive interrogation of Cunliffe, Delabier and Massey, and all their known contacts would be checked and similarly interrogated.

'A real grill?' the Commissioner asked.

'The hottest ever, sir.'

The Commissioner nodded, glanced around the set faces of the brass. 'It's all we can do, gentlemen. We'll not be sitting back, I promise.'

'The armed forces?' Frazer-Petrie asked.

Commander Daintree sat on that, hard. 'At this stage, positively no, sir. Very positively no. Later perhaps, depending which way things develop. At present this is best left to us.'

'But there's a lot of ground to cover in Scotland, Commander—'

'Ground that's well known to the Scottish police forces, sir.'

'I was thinking... a Highland regiment—'

'No, sir.' Hands flat on his thighs, chin thrust forward, Daintree came down hard again. 'Big feet, bigger than coppers' even... there's *lives* at stake! I don't want parade-ground stuff, and barking sergeant-majors doing it by Queen's Regulations. I'll use *my* book, if you don't mind, sir.' He stood up, a short man, square and tough. He addressed the Commissioner. 'If there's nothing else, Sir Richard, I'll be off.'

'Off?'

'I'm booked for Edinburgh, from Gatwick. A quick visit. Then back to start the Embassy flog.' Daintree left the room briskly.

Frazer-Petrie gave a small, annoyed cough. 'Short on manners, isn't he, your man, Sir Richard? I hope he knows what he's doing.'

Sir Richard Smith, once a copper on the beat, who'd footed it before the happy days of Pandas, stared bleakly at Frazer-Petrie. 'Manners don't *always* make the man,' he said. 'Daintree knows what he's doing, better than many of us.'

* * *

With Daintree en route for Edinburgh, other men, men of experience on the hot grill, interviewed Cunliffe, Delabier and Massey in separate Pentonville rooms guarded by armed prison officers. Not surprisingly, however hot the grill, there was no help forthcoming: Cunliffe, Delabier and Massey stood only to gain from the hijack. The effort, however, had had to be made as a matter of routine. After the interrogations the three prisoners were removed separately, in closed prison vans with escort, to three separate prisons; the Moor, Durham, and Albany in the Isle of Wight—though none of this was made public.

In the meantime other officers of the Branch interrogated all known contacts of the spies. Others again questioned the passengers' families; Ernie Peach's son, the Ruffs, Mark Graham's parents ... the two sets of parents of the Larcombes, none of whom knew that Larcombe was already dead. The Misses MacBean's employers in Nottingham were interviewed, for the MacBeans appeared to have no relatives, and shared a tiny flat, keeping themselves to themselves mostly and saving to go to Scotland. Enquiries were made at various embassies—United States for the MacFees, West German for Frau Borchardt, French for Mesdemoiselles Laffont and Libersart—but all revealed no criminal connections. Most of the other passengers were solid, respectable people, owning their own homes, retired or in steady respectable jobs, the sort of people who went on coach tours. Bent connections amongst them were highly unlikely. But Daintree's branch did know its job. Before long three names stood out; Kahn, Kerrigan and Silver. Nothing known against them, but nothing known *of* them either, since the given addresses proved false, which didn't fit the pattern of the others aboard Tour Eighteen. Commander Daintree, when this was reported to him in Edinburgh, felt that it added little to his store of useful knowledge. That could change if and when any associates of Kahn, Kerrigan and Silver were found and the squeeze put on....

'So look bloody hard,' was Daintree's order.

* * *

Slow, slow behind the breakdown vehicle. Fractured fuel pipe, Harkness was to say if questioned. Behind the wheel, steering without power, Harkness reflected on the iron nerves of Kahn. If he was Kahn, this slowness would drive him bonkers in no time. If the police should swoop, they were helpless behind the tow-rope—they could hardly cast off in time to make a getaway, and he, Harkness, certainly wouldn't be busting his guts to help. Or would he? Harkness gave a sudden shiver, seeing Kahn's eyes in the rear-view mirror as the hijack boss came back up the gangway after a visit to the tiny toilet compartment. Kerrigan for one—this, Harkness knew first-hand—was a killer. He would kill again when need be, so the police, who would surely have guns in mind, wouldn't be hasty. In this situation it behoved nobody to be hasty. *Softly, softly, catchee monkey*... Harkness sweated, seeing looming death if the monkey managed to hang on to the last. Bloody hell, Harkness thought in anguish, we could still all die even with half the cops in Britain looking through the windows! The hijackers had nothing to lose now, having killed already, but a hell of a lot to gain if they could get away with it. A gold-plated life must await those three bastards, somewhere outside Britain.

Left turn, right turn, climb, descend: lovely scenery if you were in the mood. Great mountains, sky-blue lochs, deep glens of Scotland, heather, more pine, rushing, tumbling rivers gleeful over rocks, bright sun, rowan trees, more mountain-sided lochs. Behind them now and again, impatient drivers were held up, and accelerated past when possible. They were being a bloody nuisance, Harkness thought, wishing he could call out the reason why. After a while, although, God knew, he had drunk little enough the last few days, he had to go to the toilet. He said so.

Kahn said, 'Hold it, can't you?'

'I can't concentrate.'

'You don't need to.'

'You ever driven under tow? Driven a thing this big?'

Kahn swore. 'Okay, but wait. I'm not stopping here. Wait for a lay-by.'

Harkness waited. It was half an hour before they found a

lay-by. Seeing the advance sign, Kahn got up and jammed a hand on the horn, using it in a pre-arranged code. Harkness flicked left and steered in behind the tow. He got up stiffly and walked down the gangway, looking in concern at the faces of his passengers. Old Hanborough's wife looked in a bad way, he thought, all white and kind of screwed up, mouth chewing rapidly. Same with the two old ladies in black. The Ruff girl looked a mess, all blotchy . . . they all looked at him as he went by, beseeching him with their frightened eyes to do something, to help them out. He tried to smile and look cheery, but it was an immense effort even to meet the stares. He went into the toilet. Inside, he had a thought. There was a small window, frosted glass, just for ventilation purposes. Kahn would know you couldn't get out that way, but other things could. Kahn had slipped up somewhat badly, hadn't he? Excitement gripped Frank Harkness. He brought a biro from his breast pocket and tore off a couple of sheets from the roll of toilet paper. 'Help', he wrote, his hand shaking. 'South of England coach repainted maroon, renumbered AZZ 988 G, hijacked, destination not known. Help us before it is too late.' He signed it, 'Frank Harkness, driver.'

He pushed the paper into his right-hand jacket pocket: no use throwing it out here in the lay-by, one of the men could see. He would wait till he was back in the driving seat and they had some friendly people around who just might see him drop it, and pick it up. Leaving the toilet with his secret, hoping it wouldn't show in his face, he went back up the gangway and got behind the wheel again. They pulled back on to the road and continued with their journey as before through scenery that would normally have set the heart aglow, and more piled-up traffic. A nosing police patrol appeared from ahead and passed them just a few minutes after the lay-by. Its crew gave them sweeping looks, but faded away behind. Harkness hadn't used his toilet-paper message—Kahn's eye had been too watchful. Farther on, when they had joined a main road signposted for Pitlochry, another police patrol came up fast from behind, slowed for a look, saw Rubery's fake patrol ahead, slowed again for a word, then swept on, losing no time. A little later Harkness got fresh route orders: left turn ahead for Aberfeldy. Behind the towing vehicle, behind the uniformed Rubery, the coach went on down a twisting road, largely tree-lined. The weather was still fine and clear and crisp, with a climbing sun. In the distance now and again they saw mountain tops, high and magnificent. Soon they entered the small town of Aberfeldy. Here their slow progress was slowed even more, for a pipe band was marching and there was a crowd in the roadway. The pipers were playing *Scotland the Brave*. Harkness recognized the tartan of the Black Watch and remembered the spiel he would have given over the Tannoy in easier circumstances. He would have told his passengers that here in Aberfeldy had been held, back in 1740, the first muster of the Black Watch, the Royal Highland Regiment formed from the ten independent companies of the dark-uniformed Watch over the Highlands.... As the brave skirl of the pipes and the beat of the drummers came back strongly, a glint of mischief appeared in the eye of Kahn behind Harkness, and he turned in his seat, half rising to address the passengers. 'You're on a tour of Scotland, aren't you?' he called. 'Right ahead of us is romance—one of the sights and sounds you came to see and hear, right? So what do you do?'

Silence. Silence and stares.

Kahn smiled. 'You bloody sing,' he stated. 'So sing, you bastards! The tune is *Scotland the Brave*. Sing it!'

They did. It was the Misses MacBean who got them going, the Misses MacBean who, after exchanging glances, stood in their seats and metaphorically opened their chests, seeming to gain immediate spirit and comfort from the words.

> Land of the bog and heather,
> Land of the rolling river,
> Land of my heart forever,
> Scotland the Brave...

Thus noisily, they moved through Aberfeldy, stirred, despite themselves, by their own sound, however morose their faces—all except Mesdemoiselles Laffont and Libersart, who could be seen talking all through it. As they moved on behind the pipers, the people of Aberfeldy waved at them. Some waved back: Kahn, Kerrigan and Silver, smiling. The Misses MacBean were too busy to wave: they were red in the face, bellowing, standing like soldiers themselves, staring into the face of the enemy, mouths opening and shutting like salmon, spectacles agleam with emotion. They sang and sang, verse after verse, and were through Aberfeldy before they knew it. In point of fact the coach turned off behind the pipes and drums, leaving them to march ahead and away. It turned right a little way beyond the Breadalbane Arms Hotel, down a quiet road, past the Black Watch memorial and over General Wade's bridge, taking the road to Loch Tummel. The Misses MacBean, knowing their territory and having got the bit between their teeth, sang bravely on, lifting hearts.

By Tummel, and Loch Rannoch, and Lochaber I will go,
By heather tracks wi' heaven in their wiles...

Kahn stood, put up a hand. 'That's enough,' he called.

...and if you're thinking in your inner heart
Braggart's in my step, you've never—

'*Shut it!*' Down the gangway went Kahn, looking vicious. He didn't want to overdo the infusion of spirit. 'You sing when I say, and you shut up when I say.' He reached the MacBean women and shoved the nearer one down in her seat. She plumped down sharp and sudden, looking outraged and scarlet. Grinning, Kahn went back up the coach. They went on behind the safety of the escort. No lingering in Tummel Bridge: they moved through towards Kinloch Rannoch. Between Dalriach and Balliemore they passed another police patrol and this time the convoy was stopped. An apparently satisfactory conversation took place between Rubery and the real cops, for they were all smiles and good cheer; but a real cop got out of his car and came across for a word with Harkness. As the officer approached, Harkness thrust his hand into his pocket and tried to look unconcerned and cool, very conscious of Kahn right behind him, Kahn well and truly on the ball. The policeman asked, 'Where from, driver?'

'London, East Ham.'

'On tour, I'm told.'

Harkness nodded. The policeman craned his neck, looking along the windows. Harkness thought of Kahn's gun, and Kerrigan's, and Silver's. That cop just didn't know how close he was coming, not only to God, but to the truth as well. All guns in the coach were ready, and Rubery would deal with the other cop before he'd had a chance to call his station sergeant on the radio. The cop said, 'We're looking for a blue and gold coach belonging to South of England Motor Services.' He gave the registration number. 'Don't happen to know the driver, I suppose? Name of Harkness?'

'I know lots of drivers down that way... South of England Motor Services, that's a London firm, Hounslow,' Harkness said slowly, playing hard for time. He was aware of Kahn behind, could almost feel his presence. Doing his best to keep cool, he brought his right hand from his pocket. At that moment, Kahn rose in the seat behind, stepped into the gangway and leaned across Harkness. Meeting his eye, Harkness read the message in it: something had been seen in his hand. Kahn's right hand was in his pocket. The other cop, the driver of the genuine patrol car, was coming across now and Kerrigan was poised ready. Harkness sweated: if he passed that piece of paper now, both cops would die and the coach would move on out behind its cover, still anonymous, no connections known. *Nothing would be achieved—bloody nothing!* Harkness gave a low sound of frustration and pushed his hand back into his pocket. Kahn, showing an interest, smiled down at the policeman.

'What's up?' he asked. 'Looking for the one that got away? The hijack coach?' He added, 'Heard it on the BBC.'

'That's right.' The policeman looked at Harkness again. 'I'm told,' he said, jerking a hand towards Rubery, 'you spent last night at Kirriemuir, the night before at Edinburgh. Right?'

'Right, officer.'

'Seen nothing all the way—any of South of England's coaches at all?'

Harkness slowly shook his head. 'No . . . not that I noted, like. Sorry.'

'It's okay, we'll get them. Just keep your eyes open, will you? Specially after you're on your own again. Fuel pipe fractured, isn't it?'

Harkness nodded, longing to speak out. Help, friendliness, would soon be gone now.

'Bad luck for your passengers, that, and a long way to go for a repair.' The policeman slapped the side of the coach. 'Off you go, and good luck.'

'Thanks.'

'If you happen to see a coach that fits, contact the nearest police officer, all right? The one we're after is carrying thirty-one passengers, like you, and they're all in extreme danger. Any help we can get—you know?' He looked grim.

'Sure,' Harkness said with a lump in his throat and his bowels loose as porridge. 'I'll remember, officer.' He waved to the towing driver and to Rubery waiting with his flashing blue light. They moved out, slow and ponderous, heading west. When they had cleared the cop car, there was a reaction from the passengers, a sound of women in tears, of old Hanborough fizzing like a fuse. Harkness, glancing sideways at Hanborough, knew the old man was no coward: like Harkness himself, he'd had to weigh things up and reject any stupidly pointless sacrifices. He'd been watched by Kerrigan throughout and that was that: as for physical diversions, personal attacks on gunmen, he simply wasn't capable any more. The Lancer days were long, long past. Harkness, in that glance towards Hanborough, met Kahn's eye signalling danger. Kahn gave a nasty smile with no humour in it and said, 'That pocket, friend. What you brought out before, you bring out again now.'

'There wasn't anything.'

Kahn moved. He swung round on Lady Hanborough. He seized her shoulders, thin and scraggy like her husband's, sent her backwards and forwards so that her head moved like a broken doll's, smashing backwards into the seat-top. Old Hanborough beat at him frenziedly, but Kahn didn't seem to notice. Harkness shouted, 'All right, all right!' Kahn let go of the old woman and Harkness reached once more into his pocket and brought out the toilet paper. Kahn read it, burnt it in the flame of a gas lighter, and let the charred remnant drop underfoot. He looked at Harkness. 'You'll be paying for that later,' he said. 'From now on out, no-one uses the toilet without me or Kerrigan or Silver there to watch.' He resumed his seat. Down the gangway the Americans, the MacFees, were talking again about their embassy, talking loudly in the hopes of putting the wind up Kahn. Some people, Harkness thought, never learned: and realized, with a rush of blood to the head, that the same might be said of himself. Behind the breakdown lorry, the coach turned right by Balliemore, eschewing Kinloch Rannoch, on to a road that led back up to the main A9. But, it seemed, they were not bound that far. The escort pulled off up a rutted track and into a farm where, in a large yard, a deep barn was standing open. Harkness was told to reverse into this barn. Kerrigan jumped down and disappeared. Inside two minutes he was back with another man, who climbed up for a word with Kahn.

'Everything okay?'

'Sure. Your end too?'

The newcomer nodded. He was a big-built man with a bald head and thick lips, lips red like a ripe cherry. 'The police have covered us already—no more worries, not for a while anyway.' He studied Kahn. 'You look tired. There's a bed waiting. You'll take it in spells?'

Kahn said, 'Yes, and to keep up the strength I'd like you to arrange a substitute for whoever's using the bed.' He looked around at the haunted, news-hungry passengers' faces. 'I'm taking no chances now. Any word from Glasgow?'

'No, nothing yet. Give them time. I'm not worried.' Like Kahn, the big man looked round at the passengers. 'Which is Hanborough?'

Kahn grinned. 'Need you ask? There.'

The big man looked down at the thin old man, the yellow-white moustache, the direct and bulging blue eyes. He nodded, as if answering some inner thought, absently. Kahn asked, 'Do you want him now?'

'Later.' The big man glanced at his watch, the strap only just meeting around a thick wrist. After a muttered word with Kahn, he left the coach. As he went out of the barn, the big doors were shut behind him: Harkness, through his open driving window, heard bolts being shot across. As the doors had shut, Kahn had flicked on one inside light: the result was dim, like it had been back in the forest. Kahn looked down at Harkness: Harkness, expecting retribution for his attempt at message-passing, flinched, but met his eye. Kahn said, 'All right, Harkness, I'm not a vindictive man. I'll let it pass, this time. Not again. Understand?'

Harkness nodded. They sat in silence, waiting for something else to happen. After half an hour the doors opened again and two men entered the barn, bearing food and water. Fresh-baked bread—wholesome, crusty—cheese and apples. Those who could eat, ate. All drank thirstily. When the meal was over, the barn doors opened again and the big man came back and called up to Kahn.

'I'll take them along now.'

'Hanborough?'

'And his lady wife.' There was menace in the big man's voice. He peered up from ground level, leering at the old couple. 'Come along now, my lord and my lady, there's work to be done.'

Harkness was watching: old Hanborough's face was ghastly in the dim light, all blotchy, mottled with bright red patches. He began a pathetic sort of bluster, but soon read in the big man's eyes that he was simply making a fool of himself. Harkness saw him make an effort, saw a look of *noblesse oblige* come into the wan face, saw the aged backbone stiffen militarily. One didn't run from the enemy, one fought him as long as possible, and when the time came to hand over one's sword one did it with dignity. And it was with dignity that old Hanborough, Colonel of Lancers, peer of the realm, pulled himself to his feet, using the handrail in front of him, and then bent to offer his helping arm to his wife. 'Come along, Edie,' he said simply. 'We're wanted, and we must go. Who knows, we may be able to help.'

There was a dead silence in the coach as they descended and went out of the barn with the big man.

6

AT 1800 hours the Hanboroughs had not returned; a few minutes earlier Kahn, who had allowed Silver the first bed-rest period and was on guard with Kerrigan and a man from the farm outfit, had switched on his small radio. The BBC News indicated no progress in the search for Tour Eighteen, but there was an underlying optimism that suggested the hijackers couldn't possibly get away with it. All Scotland was being toothcombed, the border roads into England, all of them, were sealed off and every heavy vehicle was being stopped and searched. Kerrigan didn't like this: he muttered into the ear of Kahn, saying this indicated that the authorities were taking into account the possibility of the passengers having been transferred. Kahn wasn't worried: they were, he said, still okay with a cop car in front, and there wasn't much more ground to cover up to the end anyway.

'Farther than we came today,' Kerrigan said.

'Sure. But it'll be fast. It's time, not distance, that'll count.' Kahn was confident, no doubts at all. Harkness wondered why this should be so; let him, if he wished, have all the confidence in the world that his victims wouldn't be cut out from under him—but what made him so sure the authorities would accede to his demands? In his very guts Harkness was quite certain they would not. What did one coach, one driver, thirty-one assorted passengers of no importance to anyone but their families amount to when set against the vital knowledge, not yet outdated, held by Cunliffe, Delabier and Massey? Put in a nutshell, the country simply could not afford to let the hostages live. The emphasis had to be on rescue, but what would Kahn, Kerrigan and Silver—and the others, those fake cops—do when rescue loomed, if ever it did?

* * *

In Edinburgh Commander Daintree, in company with police brass from all over Scotland, looked with a touch of despair which he managed to keep hidden, at a vast map covering a whole wall.

He said, 'Needle in a haystack. I'm sorry to be unoriginal, but there it is. In a sense, we don't know what we're looking for, do we?'

'You mean if they've transferred?'

Absently, Daintree nodded at the man who had spoken—Edinburgh's own police chief. 'I've a feeling they've done just that.'

'If they have, where's the original coach? We've still to find that.'

Daintree said, 'Aside from fingerprints, does it matter? Even fingerprints... they could tell us who the hijackers are, certainly. But so what? That doesn't help us get the passengers out, Mr Fortescue.' He turned back to the map: north of Perth, there were not so many roads in Scotland: it ought not really to be such a haystack if the coach, or whatever the vehicle might now be, was on the road. Almost certainly it was not, in which case they were back with the haystack again. During the day, shoals of reports had come in from the various police districts; false sightings by the public largely, but some of the police observations stood out and might prove interesting. Way up north in Caithness a coach had been found empty in a lay-by—a 31-seater, green not blue and gold, and with the wrong number. But its emptiness was intriguing, and a police patrol was standing by while another searched bleak countryside for the occupants. Closer at hand in Perthshire a patrol had reported encountering a 31-seater under tow, suffering from a fractured fuel pipe and attended by another patrol from Aberdeenshire. Over by the Clyde yet another 31-seater had been found with its nose buried in the stonework of a bridge near a waterfall. The coach was far from empty. Apart from a shaken driver there was a crowd of anxious passengers that included one face known, as it happened, to the patrol that had found the accident: a young man not long out of Barlinnie gaol, and it was interesting to ponder on why *he* should be touring round his own part of the world. Over on

Deeside, the tracks of a very heavy vehicle, identified as a coach, had been found leading up a ride in thick forest, and near the end of the ride was a clearing with evidence of fresh branch cutting and more tracks, deep ones as though the heavy vehicle had come to rest there. This was the most interesting of all, and currently the area was under intensive search. A further report was awaited.

Daintree was about to ask if in fact anything more had been heard from this area when a telephone rang. A Chief Inspector took the call, spoke briefly, glanced at Daintree and put his hand over the mouthpiece. 'For you, sir.'

'Who is it?'

'A man's voice, sir—he won't give his name.'

Daintree stiffened. 'Asking for me personally, by name?'

'Yes, sir.'

'Put a check on the line.' He indicated another phone. 'Listen yourself too.' He moved towards the first phone and took it from the Chief Inspector. 'Yes? This is Commander Daintree.' As he listened, there was a tense silence in the room. Daintree's face was expressionless, but there was a tautness about the man that spoke of developments coming along the wire. He said just the one word: 'Hanborough?' The Chief Inspector, listening too, reached out for a file on the long table, opened it, thrust it at the brass. Necks were craned: the name was there, in Tour Eighteen's nominal roll. They all looked at Daintree. After an interval Daintree spoke again. 'Noted. But you mustn't expect too much. I'm sorry. How are you all?' He listened again, his face grave. After a while he said, 'We're going to get to you, never fear. Yes, your message will be passed on, of course, but I—'

He broke off, jerked the handset from his ear and set it back on its rest. He looked up, stroking a long chin. 'Hanborough—*Lord* Hanborough. Well—we know about him, of course. Contact's now been made, which I suppose is a step in the right direction.' An internal line buzzed. He answered, nodded and said, 'Thank you.' Addressing the others, he said, 'They found the call. Call-box—naturally—in Inverness. Which we can take it is just where they won't be. But—'

'But still in Scotland.'

'Still in Scotland, yes.' Daintree's voice was quiet. 'Hanborough... he's been told to give a message for onward transmission to the Prime Minister. The hijackers mean to go through with this, and the passengers will positively die if their demands are not met. Lord Hanborough sounded quite convinced of this. He's been a soldier—he wouldn't cave in easily. But he was imploring me to act, imploring me to save all those lives. I confess—actually to speak to one of those passengers—it shook me. It's come closer home.'

There was a silence.

Daintree shrugged, became crisper again. 'I shall pass the message via Scotland Yard, gentlemen. It's up to the Prime Minister and the Cabinet, of course—but I'm not so sure when it comes to the crunch that we can set military secrets against human flesh and blood. Military secrets are susceptible to rapid change at the best of times. On the other hand...'

'Well?'

Again Daintree shrugged, then gave a tight smile. 'It could be a time'll come for subterfuge,' he said.

* * *

Old Hanborough was returned to the barn at a little after 19.30 hours. The doors were opened up and he was pushed in by the big man. Once in the barn, and caught in the long beam of Kahn's torch, he collapsed, gibbering. Lady Hanborough was with him, her face and eyes puffy with tears and blows. There was heavy bruising. Somehow she remained on her feet and called for someone to help her husband. Harkness said in a hard voice, 'I'm going and to hell with you lot,' and he got up from his seat and out of the coach, with no protest from Kahn, who accompanied him with his gun. The American also got down—MacFee, with again no protest. They bent over Hanborough: he had fainted and was out cold, but apparently unharmed physically. Harkness and MacFee lifted him gently and carried him between them, with his feet dragging through straw and muck, towards the coach. Up top one of the transistor players, Peter Brewster, squatted on the floor and reached out, taking Hanborough under the armpits and heaving. Hanborough came up with a rush, pushed from behind, and was laid as flat as possible along his and his wife's seat, long legs and arms dangling. Harkness got Lady Hanborough into his own seat and remained standing, feeling sick inside. Lady Hanborough sat quite still, quite silent like the two old ladies in black, with tears pouring down seamed, bruised cheeks. All they could do was leave her. After a couple of minutes the old man came round. He opened his eyes and stared blankly, seeming to see nothing. He talked in a far-away voice, blaming himself for something, something unmanly and unsoldierly. 'They made me do it,' he said time and again. 'They made me do it and they kept hitting Edie.' Harkness shivered at his tone, at his collapse into total helplessness. Why didn't someone, why didn't he, Harkness, fight back, make an attempt to bring one of the gunmen down? It was shameful, but those guns, and all the circumstances of the hijack, had made cowards of them all. He wondered what it was Hanborough had been made to do but knew he would have to go on wondering. Hanborough gave no clues, just kept on and on with his parrot-cry till it drove Harkness mad; and Kahn wouldn't utter. Nor did the late BBC News have anything to satisfy curiosity.

That night there was one further development: the towing vehicle, already cast off from Tour Eighteen's front, was trundled out of the barn, to be replaced a few minutes later by another police patrol car, complete with more policemen, Rubery style. Down in the barn there was low talk with the big man, who had taken over the guard from Kahn, and then the new arrivals went outside, presumably to bed, leaving their car hidden in the barn. The big man got back in and, keeping his gun nicely in view, leaned across the handrail over old Hanborough, looking down the dimly lit gangway. Hanborough was still stretched out and was now, at long last, sleeping. His wife still occupied the driving seat. Harkness was now berthed with Ernie Peach, whose wife Elsie was remaining with Susan Larcombe. Harkness and Ernie, neither of whom could sleep, talked in low voices, sharing their minds, putting into words the terrible mental stress of these last days. Harkness was trying to formulate something, some kind of strike-back. Ernie, a small man but pugnacious, was all for it —but always provided his wife didn't get hurt. That was the ever-present trouble: almost everybody had somebody that mattered more than they did themselves. 'Except those two youngsters,' Ernie Peach whispered in Harkness's ear. 'Not brothers or anything, are they?'

'No ... Brewster and Hurst. Could be cousins, I suppose.'

'I'd say it's up to them, wouldn't you?'

'It's hard to decide for other folk, Mr Peach, very hard. Hard to know the thing to *do*, too.'

'Grab one of the buggers with guns. . . .'

'And wait for the other two to start shooting?' Harkness shook his head. 'They're professionals, we're not! Someone's bound to get hurt. And a touring car—a coach—well, it's not laid out for what you might call a concerted attack. Takes time to pull yourself out of the seats into the gangway—too much bloody time, and not enough bloody room.'

'I think,' Ernie Peach said, 'we've *got* to take a risk before long. I said about Elsie—about my wife. Well, that stands. But in the long run—if we don't get out—well!' He didn't want to put it into words: it was too close, too appallingly real, that they were all going to die. It was a funny thing, Harkness thought glumly, but from the snatches of conversation he'd overheard, everyone aboard seemed to be taking it for granted that the hijackers meant what they said, and that the law would never find them in time. After a while Peach made a concrete suggestion: what if something went wrong with the engine? Couldn't Harkness fix that somehow?

'I've thought of that too,' Harkness said, 'but I doubt if I could fool them. They'll know about engines.'

'I mean for real.'

'Yes. Thought about that, too! There's things I could do ... but they have resources. They'd just whistle up another vehicle, I reckon.' Nevertheless, it could be worth more thought. If he could achieve a bust engine at just the right moment—when it was too late for a substitution—it would certainly cause a panic. The risk to life and limb would be high; but no harm in trying to think something up along those lines, just in case . . .

After a time, they fell into sleep, uneasily, uncomfortably.

* * *

At the back, Kerrigan was on watch. One of the farm men, relieving Silver, was up front with his big, bald boss. Kerrigan was watching the seat a little way up on the left: Jilly Ruff's hair was falling over the arm rest and dangling into the gangway, making Kerrigan's mind wander along its set paths and making his flesh react. He had an inflamed sort of feeling inside his head, and his brain felt light, floating. Something had to be done about it. Kerrigan ran his tongue over his lips, ran his mind over the days ahead: in the coach till the Monday deadline, after that in the aircraft with Kahn and Silver, Rubery and the men dressed as cops, plus Cunliffe, Delabier and Massey. All those people shared one thing—their sex. There would be no women. Where the aircraft was flying to, at any rate in the first instance, life would also lack women. It might be a long, long while before Kerrigan had it off. He sat there scowling, thinking, nursing his gun. Tonight was as good a time as any—while Kahn was asleep in the farm house there was a certain latitude that might not occur again. Next time Kahn was off watch, so might Kerrigan be, and the chance would be lost...

After an interval, Kerrigan, his eyes burning like fever, got up. He walked along the gangway, and spoke to the big man. 'Going into the house,' he said, moistening his lips again. 'You and your bloke okay for a few minutes?'

The big man nodded. 'Don't linger, though. What d'you want in the house?'

'A word with Kahn.'

'He's asleep.'

'I know. He won't mind.'

'On your head be it,' the big man said, grinning. Kerrigan got down, slipped out of the barn through a trap door used by hens, the main doors being still barred from the outside. Five minutes later he was back and climbing into the coach. 'Kahn,' he said to the big man, 'wants...' His voice trailed off. In that dim light he had seen Susan Larcombe, seen the

sheen of the fair hair, the rather elf-like, triangular face...
the dumb girl, the extra thrill ... and easier to bring out without fuss than Jilly Ruff, for Jilly had her man with her, whereas the dumb one ... His voice hoarse, Kerrigan finished addressing the big man. 'Kahn wants the Larcombe girl.' He breathed hard and his eyes glistened.

The big man looked into his face and smiled softly. 'Does he now?'

'That's what he said.' Kerrigan was blustering.

'What for? Or shall I guess?' The smile grew softer. 'Not for that. Oh, I know Kahn, he's single-minded. The job's the job, Mr Kerrigan, as well you know. Women are for afters—that's a strict rule with Kahn. So?'

'So what?' Kerrigan looked blank.

'So you aim to have her for yourself—right?'

'No skin off your nose,' Kerrigan said, making his admission, his face red with anger, with frustration.

'No? I'm human too. I can make trouble for you, unless...'

'Unless what?'

The smile was bland now. 'Unless we share.'

Kerrigan hesitated. 'If we do?'

'They're asleep—mostly, anyway. They won't know, and I'll say nothing to Kahn.' Their eyes met. They each knew the score: Kahn would be told anyway; even if the passengers were all asleep, which they in fact were not, they would wake with their eyes on stalks and their ears flapping—yes, Kahn would be told, but by then it would be a *fait accompli* and meantime Kerrigan's need was urgent, too urgent to be put off. But if he didn't go along with the big man, there would be, simply, no oats. He read that plain.

He said, 'Okay, then.'

They approached Susan, who was asleep. So was Elsie Peach, but she woke when Kerrigan leaned across, woke startled. Kerrigan shushed at her. 'Kahn wants the girl. She'll soon be back.'

'You—'

'Shut up. Or I'll shut you up for good and all.' Kerrigan prodded with his gun. Susan was awake now, eyelids fluttering, face frightened. 'Come along now,' Kerrigan said, showing his teeth. 'Don't be scared. It's just that Kahn wants a word, that's all.' He pulled her to her feet. Between them, he and the big man got her out into the gangway and moved towards the door, but not unseen. There was an interruption: the American, MacFee.

'Hey! What's going on?' The fleshy round face was leant out into the gangway, staring, the spectacles reflecting the overhead light.

Kerrigan turned. 'Nothing's going on. What's it to do with you anyway? You just do as you're told, nothing more.'

'But that girl... gee, she's—'

Now they were all waking up: sleep had been shallow enough as it was, they were all suffering with shattered nerves, agog, responsive to the least sound. Foul language came from Kerrigan, but he was stopped in mid-stream by the big man. 'It's no good, Kerrigan, leave it.'

'I'm—'

'I said, leave it!' The heavy face loomed threateningly. 'We'll have the bloody place in an uproar—and Kahn's not going to like it. Specially leaving just one man on watch, Kerrigan.' He reached out, grasped the tense body and shook it. 'Kerrigan, see sense!'

Kerrigan swung round, holding Susan. He gave her a hard push, back into her seat so that she fell over Elsie Peach. His face livid, he moved down the coach and stopped alongside MacFee. Given immense strength by his rage, he dragged the American out into the gangway by his hair, butted him in the stomach and smashed him down flat on the floor. Then he put the boot in right where it hurt the most, time after time till he was dragged away by the big man.

Harkness watched from his seat, hating himself. The chance had been missed: the taste was bitter in his mouth.

7

IN THE morning, up front, old Hanborough was still sleeping and snoring. It seemed nothing would wake him. This, in any event, no-one tried to do: he might resume his dreadful keening. Nerves rubbed raw couldn't take too much of that kind of irritation, however much the sympathy for the old man. Farther down the coach the two French women, Mesdemoiselles Laffont and Libersart, who for so long had talked in their own language, were now silent, sitting and staring with angry eyes, their faces seeming to accuse everybody, all their fellow passengers, of being in the plot against them. Just in front of them Frau Borchardt, the German woman, sat impassive, like the two old ladies in black, but more formidable, as though she had not surrendered at all but was merely waiting for her moment to fight for *Lebensraum*.

Jilly Ruff thought ceaselessly of home. Mark Graham had lost his power to comfort her now: he was the one who had taken her away, the one responsible for all this. Thoughts of Mum and Dad, the square house with its square patch of garden, Horsham itself, filled all her waking hours now and these things all seemed so close at times that she felt she could almost reach out and grasp them; but then she was cruelly jolted back to the present reality of the dim light, the silent coach, the enclosing barn, and Kerrigan's frustrated face. Small things came back to her, silly things; the way her father pushed his top dentures out with his tongue, searching beneath the plate after meals; the look on Mum's face when, spoken to in the evenings, she wasn't really listening but was counting stitches—you could always tell, because she waggled her nose in time with the counting; the way Dad put the paper up and sort of crackled it angrily when Mum yacked at him. She thought of her bedroom, all her possessions that she wouldn't see again. Silently, tears spilled from her eyes and rolled down her cheeks, a bitter salty trail.

It was now Thursday morning: less than four days to go.

* * *

Daintree, on that Thursday morning, was back in London: he had just wanted to get the feel of things in Scotland, use his presence briefly to ensure the pulling out of all the stops. He was glad enough that this hadn't in the event been necessary: the hunt was in good hands. He arrived in his office tired but brisk and called for a cup of black coffee. Before bringing it his secretary handed him a sealed envelope from Frazer-Petrie of the Cabinet Office. This he ripped open. The note was brief: the Prime Minister had considered Lord Hanborough's plea but saw no reason to change his mind.

Daintree drummed his fingers on his desk-top. Aloud, in a bitterness of spirit, he said, 'So they all die ... all of them. Poor bastards!' He got up with an abrupt movement, almost a savage one, pushing his chair back and going over to a window, set high over London. He stared down into Victoria Street filled with busy cars, buses, taxis, lorries, looked along towards Westminster Cathedral's immense red-brick pile and tower and left towards the Abbey, the House of Commons, the rolling London River swelling unconcernedly beneath the bridges. Not so far behind his back lay Buckingham Palace, Wellington Barracks, the Horse Guards ... Daintree thought of all these things and turned as his secretary came in with coffee. 'Thank you, Miss Colville,' he said. He didn't use Christian names, his position was a vulnerable one: he was one of the men who, when necessary, had to investigate ministers of the Crown whose peccadilloes made them a security risk. He swept an arm around, indicating the view from the window. 'D'you ever think about all that?' he asked.

'Think about what, Commander?' The girl smiled. 'I'm not a very willing Londoner!'

Daintree nodded, smiled back absently. 'Maybe not. Nor me. Give me the open country, Yorkshire... But it does no harm to think about the past, London's past, at times. The river—Britain's greatness. All that commerce, the great ships, the warehouses down river from Tower Bridge, the comings and goings to and from all the world. Parliament...the sheer power—once—of the British Parliament! The Queen. The British Navy. The Brigade of Guards. Victory in every war we ever fought—bar the Americans!' He added with apparent inconsequence, 'American's involved in this too— at least, three of her nationals are.'

The girl was puzzled. 'I don't get it,' she said.

Daintree waved his arm again. 'I said—think! I've thought, and I admit I don't like it. All that out there, all I've just said. Army, Navy, Air Force...what's the use? We're powerless! A bunch of bloody brigands take a coach from under our noses and we're helpless, can't fight back! God, what's gone wrong with the world?'

He drank his coffee.

* * *

The little outburst had helped: Daintree had released some pressure. Later that morning he was engaged in what he had referred to as 'the Embassy flog'. He had his private contacts and he used them. He made a telephone call and at 11.30 he was sitting on a bench in Victoria Station, reading the *Daily Express* sports page. Unfortunately, an elderly woman had plumped down with a heavy suitcase next to him: he cursed her silently when he saw his contact approaching from the Gents. A thin man, middle-aged, dark with a Latin look. Daintree got to his feet and moved out from the ranks of dirty benches towards Smith's bookstall. The thin man saw him, watched him without looking as though he was doing so. Daintree glanced over the paperbacks and the magazines, blew out his cheeks, turned his back on Smith's, glanced up at the clock, and wandered towards the bar in the corner of the station concourse. The thin man drifted, bought some cigarettes at the kiosk, lit one with a match which he threw away, looked at his watch, shrugged, and also went into the bar. Daintree was buying a Scotch: the thin man did likewise. They ended up at separate but adjoining small tables, down the far end. Daintree spread out the *Daily Express*, the thin man opened a *Daily Telegraph*. Daintree, thinking once again about the past might of Britain, started the conversation.

'The missing coach.'

There was an indistinct sound from the thin man.

'You've heard who they want?'

A sound of assent.

'A Moscow involvement seems likely, more than likely. Any comment?'

A pause. 'I don't know.'

'You're in touch. Find out, will you?'

'Do what I can.'

Moodily, Daintree drank his whisky and went to the bar for another. When he got back to his table, the thin man had gone. Daintree didn't want the second drink, and time was pressing, but you couldn't be too careful. He drank slowly, then left, walked briskly along Victoria Street, back to the Yard. He buzzed for his Number Two, a chief superintendent. Within half a minute there was a knock at the door, which opened.

'Morning, Ramsey. About Kahn, Kerrigan and Silver. Anything emerged yet?'

'It's been reported to you, hasn't it—no form?'

Daintree nodded. 'It has. I want to know their background.'

'Yes, sir. Well, I—'

'Sit down, Ramsey.'

Ramsey sat. 'The names appear genuine, but not the addresses—'

'This I know too. How d'you know the names are genuine?'

Ramsey smiled. 'We've not wasted time, sir.'

'I'm glad to hear that,' Daintree said tartly.

'Yes, sir. Following certain lines of theory, two of our lads have found associates of the man Kahn, also of the man Kerrigan. Not, as yet, Silver. Silver boarded the coach in Nottingham, and he doesn't appear to be known at what we might call the London end. However, since Kahn and Kerrigan are using genuine names, it seems likely Silver is too—'

'Yes, yes, all right. When did you learn this?'

'Only a matter of minutes before you buzzed for me. Our man had just reported in. He reported that neither Kahn nor Kerrigan had precise means of livelihood, though both appeared to have money enough. They were both known—a little pressure was applied—to have gone on holiday together.'

Daintree said, 'I don't see that it helps much—not yet. These associates. What are they—ex-cons?'

'Yes, sir.'

'Are they likely to cough further?'

'We can only hope. We'll be trying.'

'Where are they now, Ramsey? On the loose?'

There was a grin from the Chief Superintendent. 'Oh no, sir. Helping us with our enquiries.'

'Can you spin it out till Monday?'

Ramsey nodded. 'Yes, I can. I doubt if they're directly involved, though, so we'll not be able to hold them after that—'

Daintree interrupted brusequly. 'I don't give a damn about after that, Chief Superintendent, just so long as we get Kahn, Kerrigan and Silver in the net in time. I think I'll have a word with these associates myself.' He added, 'After that, I'm going to have a personal go at Cunliffe, Delabier and Massey—and *their* associates.'

* * *

There was nothing to be gained from the associates of Kahn, Kerrigan or Silver. Just nothing. Daintree tried all he knew, dire threats included: the men he interviewed all had form, mostly for armed robbery. Since they had almost certainly gone back to their work after coming out of prison, they could be considered susceptible to the squeeze, but cough anything they would not. Yes, they knew the men they were being questioned about; yes, there had been an involvement on certain past jobs; yes, they had gone away on holiday, destination unknown. They didn't know anything about political involvements. At the end of long separate sessions, Daintree felt drained empty. He was inclined to believe the men—there were two women as well, who were no more help, they'd just been passing bed-mates—and at the end of it he changed his original intention. He wasn't naive enough to think that any threat to old pals would shift the plans of Kahn, Kerrigan and Silver. He told Ramsey to turn them all loose.

'But tail them,' he said savagely, sceptical of results. 'Tail them and don't lose them. Don't let 'em even go to the lavatory without you knowing.'

By this time it was evening, Thursday evening: time was shortening, going too fast now. Daintree didn't spare himself, didn't even wait for a meal. He was helicoptered direct to the maximum-security Albany prison. Insisting on doing this his way, he talked to Cunliffe from behind a bright light, his own face invisible, with two prison officers on the door. Violence he couldn't use, but violence was in him and it came out in his voice, in his approach.

'You're a bastard, Cunliffe. You're a spy. You sold your country. Who's working for you now, who's hoping to get you out?'

No answer: just a wary look from hooded eyes, the eyes of a scientist.

'Delabier says, Moscow.'

A smile. 'Delabier wouldn't say that.'

Delabier hadn't; but the point was so obvious, in Daintree's mind, that it was not especially important to pursue it. He changed his tack. 'Tell me about Kahn, Kerrigan and Silver.'

'I don't know them.'

'You know them, all right.'

Another smile. 'I suppose Delabier does?'

Daintree wanted to do a real wartime interrogation—fists, rubber tubing, boots in the right place, the one and only. Silently he cursed convention, cursed—now—even the right of cons to complain. He snarled. 'You won't find it a bed of roses in Russia, Cunliffe.'

'Admitting defeat, are you?'

God ... the damned confidence, the insolence!

Daintree controlled himself. 'We shall not be defeated. You will not go to Russia, you will not go anywhere.'

'You'll let those people die?'

'If it comes to that, yes. Their deaths will be on your head, Cunliffe, yours and Delabier's and Massey's. You won't have an easy time.' He leaned forward, told a barefaced lie. 'Do you know something, Cunliffe? In this very prison... here in Albany... there's a man whose mother is aboard that coach. I'm not telling you his name, of course. Well?'

The bright light shone, showing every expression on Cunliffe's face: that face had reacted in a sudden twitch, a twitch of real fear. Cunliffe, by this time, knew something of prison life. But he controlled his fear, and laughed into the invisible face of Daintree. 'Of course you won't tell me, since this man lives only in your imagination, Commander Daintree.'

'You're going to regret your disbelief. I've known men carved up for less in prison. You can save yourself, you know, Cunliffe.'

'How?'

'By talking. You might—no promises, but you might—get some extra remission... by talking, Cunliffe.'

'About what? I've already said—'

'We'll leave the question of ultimate responsibility. Frankly, I'm more interested in plans at this moment.'

'Plans?'

'Which airfield it's to be, where the coach will be at that time, exactly what they mean to do. Don't tell me you don't know the answers, Cunliffe.'

Once again, Cunliffe smiled. He said, 'I know as much as Delabier.'

It went on and on, quite fruitlessly. Threaten, promise, almost, in the end, plead—no use! Cunliffe was quite sure, quite confident. He wasn't going to mess things up, wasn't going to admit anything. He was sure, Daintree believed, because he was British—odd, but true! Cunliffe just could not believe any British Government in the 1970's could survive if it allowed thirty-two innocent persons to die a violent death when they could be saved almost by a stroke of the pen. Daintree had a sudden thought: why not get the Prime Minister to pay a personal visit to Albany, to the Moor, to Durham? That hard face, that granite expression that could come down like a wall when the Prime Minister was in a mean-it mood, could do nothing but wholly convince. The wide, angry eyes, the out-thrust lower lip, the backward tilt of the head... maybe a television appearance, watched by Cunliffe, Delabier and Massey by order, was the answer!

Daintree closed the interview and boarded the helicopter again for Princetown. After a talk with the Governor, he got to work on Massey: different man, but same result. Daintree felt murderous after that second interview. The Governor saw him off for Durham with concern. Daintree slept in the helicopter, woke to eat some sandwiches, and by breakfast time on Friday morning was in Durham gaol, interrogating Delabier; result, as by this time he'd known it would be, negative. Back to London, and in his office a message: the thin man he'd met yesterday morning had phoned in—would he call? Daintree did. The thin man's voice said, 'No luck. I'm sorry. No-one's talking. No interest expressed.'

Daintree rang off. There was always a difficulty in getting a line on anything Russian, and Daintree knew it. He gave a heavy sigh. Maybe it didn't matter after all. What mattered was the time. He looked at his watch: 13.15, Friday afternoon. Sixty hours to go.

8

DAINTREE, toying still with the idea of trying to persuade the Prime Minister to make a television broadcast, a statement of intent to the nation, finally and firmly rejected it. It *might* convince Cunliffe, Delabier or Massey, and they *might* then decide to talk in order to preserve themselves afterwards against their fellow prisoners. Might, might. But such a broadcast would surely worsen the lot of the men and women aboard Tour Eighteen: in fact it could be fatal. The chief aim must be to keep those people alive, and Daintree found his mind veering back towards an earlier idea: subterfuge. There were risks in that as well, one of them being that the same trick couldn't, in the sorry event of future hijacks, be played twice. But there was always the hope that to defeat the aims of the present hijackers would in itself ensure that it didn't happen again.

He put it to the Commissioner. 'Go along with them,' he suggested. 'Leak the word that we're ready to agree, at any rate, to *talk*, though that could be a waste of time—their demands aren't exactly susceptible to compromise. But if we were to move Cunliffe and the others, walk back on the segregation, get them together again, all ready for a hand-over, and then find some reason to delay until we were ready—'

'Ready to take the coach?'

Daintree said, 'Yes, sir. Without a hand-over.'

'They'll be expecting something like that.'

'Perhaps. But they can't be sure. They'll have to take a chance, won't they? They'll have to show themselves.'

'They'll show at the selected airfield, yes—or their accomplices, the receivers of the convicts if you like, will. Not the coach. They won't be driving into any traps, Daintree.'

'We'll have to find the coach, then.'

'Isn't that what we're trying to do?'

Daintree sighed. 'Yes, sir, we are. My way'll give us a little more elbow room. It's beginning to look like the only hope.'

'It smells a bit, Daintree.'

'True,' Daintree said, 'but so do the hijackers. Oh, I know what you mean, of course—the future. I've thought of that, too, but I doubt if those people aboard the coach are bothered much about any future after Monday morning. Isn't it worth at least a little consideration?'

The Commissioner got up, prowled about his office, frowning, mouth tight and hard. Swinging round on Daintree after a couple of minutes he said, 'It's been in my mind, as a matter of fact. I dare say it's been in others', but it's not yet been expressed . . .'

'Will you express it, sir?' Daintree waited, heart in mouth, convinced now that it must be done. 'Express it to the Cabinet?'

The Commissioner nodded. 'Yes, I'll do that.'

'Thank you, sir.'

'I'll put it formally to the Prime Minister himself—I'm seeing him in half an hour's time at Number 10. But don't go overboard yet, Commander. You know the Prime Minister. He's not a compromiser either, any more than the hijackers.'

* * *

It was the MacBean women who suggested singing to keep their spirits up. Not unexpectedly, it turned out they had both been Girl Guides and during the war they had both served in the Wrens. Singing, in the circumstances, was the obvious panacea, and surprisingly Kahn, when Jeanie MacBean, the elder sister, got up and made the suggestion, didn't squash it. Harkness couldn't understand that, but supposed that Kahn, when the eventual move-out came, didn't want to take to the roads with everyone looking as terrible as old Hanborough and his wife.

Kahn said, 'That's okay so long as the noise doesn't escape.

All windows tight shut.' He called to Silver. 'Rod, go outside the barn and listen, all right?'

Silver left the coach and crawled out through the hen hatch. Kahn grinned at his captives and gave a signal to the Mac-Beans. 'Okay,' he said.

They started. At first they sang alone, looking ridiculous, but sounding not untuneful. 'Underneath the spreading chestnut tree...' they sang, hopefully, going through the motions. There was a bit of a laugh, which Harkness was delighted to hear. Then he joined in with a deep bass. More and more started singing. The hen hatch door swung, and Silver came back.

'It's all right,' he said. 'You can't hear from any distance. I've got Frost to watch out for anything on the road, just in case.' Frost was the big man. 'He'll let us know.'

Kahn nodded. The MacBeans started a different song as there wasn't really room in the coach to do the motions to *Underneath the Spreading Chestnut Tree* properly. Inevitably the Misses MacBean switched to Scotland, and the passengers sang themselves through an extensive repertoire. Even Hanborough roused himself, when Scotland was at last exhausted, to start *Soldiers of the Queen*. Singing with the rest, Harkness let his mind rove over the possibility, still there in his thoughts, of doing something desperate to the coach. There were many things he could do if he ever got the opportunity The trouble was, would he? His one and only freedom came when, in company with one or other of the gunmen, he emptied the contents of the chemical lavatory in a pit dug in a field at the back of the barn, and on that unenviable trip he was hardly likely to find an excuse for opening up the engine and doing damage. Perhaps it would have to wait till they were on the road again. It could, in fact, be better then since they would be nice and obvious to any passing cops. Then he remembered Rubery's cop car, now joined by the second one. His heart sank: no other cops would intervene.

Kahn put the stopper on half way through *Soldiers of the Queen*: it was a shade too rousing. They were all sorry when it ended; it had taken their thoughts for a pleasant trip into forgetfulness. The Misses MacBean looked flushed and pleased at their success. But a blight was cast when Hanborough, who had stood for his own contribution, sat down beside his wife. Taking one alarmed look at her, he felt for her heart. His relief, when he evidently felt the beat, was pathetic, but all was far from well. Lady Hanborough's head was lolling; and suddenly, startlingly, she began breathing hard and making a curious snoring noise.

Hanborough got up again. 'My wife,' he said harshly. 'She's ill. I think she's had a stroke.'

Kahn looked down at her. 'That's too bad.'

'She must have a doctor at once!'

'Sorry. No doctors.'

'But she must!'

'No doctors,' Kahn said.

Hanborough began shaking, pleading. 'She'll die, don't you understand? *She'll die.*' He reached out towards Kahn. 'You must do something, you must telephone—'

Kahn pushed him away and he fell back against the handrail. 'She's your wife, you nurse her. There won't be any telephoning. If you weren't such a bloody old fool you'd see that for yourself. Now get on with it and stop being a nuisance.'

Hanborough wept, a terrible sight. He knelt beside his wife, took her hands, smoothed her brow. 'Edie,' he kept on saying, 'Edie my love, you mustn't leave me . . .' He was not left alone; Jeanie MacBean went to his side, murmuring comforting words which he didn't hear. Jeanie MacBean settled herself beside the old lady. Now more strain was added to the continuing ordeal as they all listened to the rasping sounds of Lady Hanborough's breathing.

* * *

Kahn was on the telephone to London, from a call-box in Pitlochry. He spoke to a man in Church Street, Kensington. 'Move as planned,' he said. 'All's well here. Your end?'

'All okay. Organizationally, that is.' There was a warning in the voice.

'Oh?'

'There's a little bird that sings of non co-operation.'
'I see. Not to worry, that'll change.'
'You sound confident?'

'Sure thing.' Kahn laughed. 'Been reading the papers, haven't you?' He rang off and went back to his car. He thought about the papers, the papers that he hadn't allowed the coach passengers to see. True, the editorials had been about ninety per cent solid for no surrender of spies—right behind the government line. But there had been the exceptions, and there had been a strong undercurrent in the news reports and the interviews with the public—on the television especially—an undercurrent, coming to the fore, that said lives must not be sacrificed, that the knowledge possessed by Cunliffe, Delabier and Massey was not all that vital. There were even signs that political capital might be made out of it, and the Prime Minister, uncompromising as he was, had never been a vote loser. Wheels within wheels . . . and many, many members of his party were more than capable of putting their careers, their seats, before the national consideration. Currently, the passengers of Tour Eighteen were of much more concern to the public than were Cunliffe, Delabier and Massey.

Kahn, driving back to the farm by Balliemore, was fully confident as to which way the wind would finally blow.

* * *

'Hang on to your hat,' the Commissioner said. 'And your blood pressure.'

Daintree waited: the Commissioner had just come back from Downing Street, looking white. He sat at his desk, put his head in his hands for a moment, then looked into Daintree's face. 'He's turned your idea down flat. Very flat—he was in a bloody awful mood.'

Daintree's stomach curdled.

'There's worse.'

'I don't think there could be, sir.'

'You wait! He's going to make a television appearance, a talk to the nation at 21.00 hours tomorrow, Saturday.'

'Oh, no!' Unbidden, Daintree sat down with a thump. 'What's he going to say . . . or can I guess?'

'I think you can. No surrender—the risk can't be taken. All possible will be done, but there'll be no surrender. He's going to enjoy being very, very British.' Bleakly, the Commissioner smiled. 'In his view, it's the equivalent of what he can no longer do—send a gunboat.' He added, 'To be fair, I gather he's got the Americans on his back. They say they're involved in radar defence as much as us. And that, God help us, happens to be true, Daintree.'

'So is the fact there are American nationals in that coach—'

'Yes, plus two French, plus one German—none of it signifies. All the governments are together on this. No surrender, and I have to see their point—up to a point! So must you, if you're to remain sane and effective, Daintree. Find that coach—that's all you can do.' He looked up. 'Any developments?'

'None, sir. I was thinking . . .'

'Yes?'

'Contrary to what I said at the start, it could be time to bring in troops.'

The Commissioner nodded. 'I agree. I'll talk to the Home Office—there'll be co-operation on that, I know.' He reached out for one of his telephones. 'As a matter of fact, that's another thing I discussed with the Prime Minister.'

* * *

The Army and the RAF were ready, expecting that in the end they would be called in. The orders went from the Defence Ministry urgently, to all home commands, and were put into immediate execution. Helicopter squadrons, some of them naval, went north into Scotland. They would co-operate to the full with the various police authorities, co-ordinated from the start of the emergency by Edinburgh. Infantry, backed by armoured columns on the ground, disgorged from the helicopters to spread out widely, leaving the machines to swoop low over the remote highland glens, seeking, peering, searching in a desperate race against time. Kahn, taking a walk outside the barn early on the Saturday morning, heard the approach of one of the helicopters. He was still standing there when it came in sight. He gave it a wave, and the pilot waved back, skimming low over the barn. There was nothing suspicious on the ground, and the machine flew away, making for Loch Rannoch. The people in the coach heard it as well, and faces grew hopeful, just for a brief spell, until they heard the sounds receding, leaving them alone in their misery.

Lady Hanborough had grown, if anything, worse: the snoring affected them all badly. Sorry as they were for the old man, they wanted nothing so much as for her to die, to be put out of her misery and for themselves to be relieved from the nerve-tearing effect of her snores. Each snore drew a groan of near dementia from Jilly Ruff: she felt she would go mad if it didn't stop soon. She tried to shut it out by burying her head in the arms of Mark Graham, to whom she had now returned as her one and only means of support, but who in fact showed every sign of being a broken reed. He was suffering badly, and had little to give anyone, even Jilly. The only one who seemed to register nothing was Susan Larcombe, withdrawn into her state of dumbness and appearing now not to hear either. Her face was a mask, white, drawn, deeply shadowed, no longer pretty. The fair hair was dank, dirty with sweat and lack of a comb. Elsie Peach, dividing her time between the girl and her own husband, was in a bad state of nerves herself. Alan, their son, would be worried stiff: the newspapers must be full of it. That was another thing that was trying—to be almost completely cut off from news of the outside world. Kahn was never communicative and the news bulletins were not always easy to hear. The passengers existed in limbo, as though they had been written off and forgotten, though the sound from the air just recently had been close enough overhead to indicate a search—so somebody, somewhere, must be doing something. Elsie Peach looked along the coach and shivered. They all looked like corpses, with nothing useful left to say. Even the speculation had stopped now: there seemed no point in it. What would happen, would happen. The air in the coach was foetid, heavy with used breath and unwashed bodies. It oppressed them all, enervated them. Elsie hoped that as the deadline approached someone would recover lost initiative. Kahn, at the start, had spoken of a big bang: if they were to be blown up anyway, they might just as well die a little earlier in an attempt to seize control.

Elsie, so far as she was able from her seat, studied the faces of the men. She found little reassurance except in just a few—those youngsters, Hurst and Brewster, more resilient because of their youth, might, she fancied, be biding their time. The driver, Mr Harkness... he had always looked dependable though he was clearly out of his depth now. He didn't look as though he would sit tamely by and be blown up, though. And her husband, Ernie. Elsie gave a fond, rather idiotic smile and felt tears start behind her eyes. Ernie was steady, phlegmatic, a real nine-to-fiver and proud of it: such men were part of the national backbone, he had always said—and she agreed. Nothing romantic about them, but where would England be without them? They provided the solid base—the taxpayers, the owner-occupiers of a more stable era, the respectable people who had a small but solid niche and who were proud of their independence. Ernie Peach was not a man of action, but Elsie had a small proud feeling that he might surprise them all in the end. Already he had given a hint or two: his mettle was up, in a quiet and unobtrusive way. He wasn't going to be sat on all the way through. She knew the savage killing of young Larcombe had affected him deeply. Since then, a bit of bulldog truculence had come into his face.

Kahn, coming back into the barn after the aerial sounds had gone, climbed up and switched on his radio, getting the BBC News. Not much was said about the hijacked coach—the authorities, Elsie thought, wouldn't be wanting to give anything away and that was natural and proper, but it did add to the cut-off, forgotten feeling. Then there was an important announcement: the newsreader put on the kind of voice that indicated weight. At 21.00 hours that night the Prime Minister would speak to the nation on all television channels.

9

IN THE farmhouse, Kahn watched the broadcast, together with Frost and Rubery. Kerrigan, Silver and one of the phoney police officers kept guard in the coach. The Prime Minister spoke from Downing Street, forearms resting on a table in front of him, hands clasped, body leaning forward powerfully. With the head held very slightly back, eyes hooded to slits stared determinedly and icily—no doubt aware that they were staring into the eyes of Kahn. The sentences, weightily delivered, seemed personally addressed. The Prime Minister was clearly, as Daintree would have had it, in a mean-it mood.

'Every means available will be used ... have no doubt, we shall find them and bring them out safely ... these wicked men must and will be punished ... we shall never give in to blackmail. There will not, I repeat, there will not, be any handing over of convicted spies. I know you, our people, would not have it otherwise.'

The image, pink flesh in a dark suit, faded out on an upthrust chin. Kahn laughed and caught Rubery's eye. 'I'm not worried,' he said.

* * *

In London, Daintree did not watch the Prime Minister: he had other things to do, and he did them. The most important was to meet, in accordance with an anonymous telephone call that had reached him in his office just an hour before the Prime Ministerial appearance, a woman who had been insistent and who had spoken good English with an accent which Daintree couldn't readily identify. He was to meet her at the home of an opposition M.P. whom he knew as a casual acquaintance, and he was to come straight away. He went in his own car, parking it some distance from the M.P.'s house in Chelsea. The M.P.'s wife, looking scared and kind of 'underground', let him in and shut the front door.

'In the study, Commander Daintree.' She showed him the door and left him to it. Then she quickly disappeared: she wasn't going to be involved. Of her husband there was no sign, but Daintree felt that his unknown telephone caller had been given some sort of accolade of genuineness.

He went into the study. A tall woman turned from the window: she was young, but not pretty. A hard face, and shrewd... big-boned and with a full round chin, a woman who one day would be a battleaxe.

'You are Commander Daintree?'

He nodded. 'And you?'

'I am Esther Marko, a second secretary in the Czechoslovak Embassy. This I shall prove.' She marched towards him, large and straight, with an almost military precision. She took a small folded card from her handbag, and opened it for him. He looked at it: it appeared genuine, and in any case he saw no reason to doubt the woman's veracity—yet.

Again he nodded. 'All right. What do you want?'

She said, 'Shall we sit down?'

They did so, in comfortable old leather arm-chairs on either side of a fireplace in front of which stood a needlework screen. She said, 'You are busy, I shall not take very long. I come about Cunliffe, Delabier and Massey. You understand, of course?'

'I know who they are,' he said cautiously.

She made a gesture of impatience. 'There is no time for fencing, Commander Daintree. We both know the facts—'

'I don't know enough of them, as it happens.'

She smiled. 'That is honest, I think, and I like it. I know it is true, also!'

'That's why I admitted it. Do I take it you've come to give me some information?'

'Yes,' she said. She seemed to be stiffening herself, renewing a resolution: there was more than a trace of fear in her eyes. Daintree felt a rising excitement, was again much aware of the shortness of the time that was left. He said gently, 'You don't want your name involved—I understand that. So far as possible, it'll be kept out of the limelight.'

'So far as possible,' she said in a low voice. 'However, I have come, and I shall speak. I feel very much for the people in the coach, Commander Daintree. That is why I am here. My parents were both killed in a hijack of an aeroplane.'

Daintree started: memory came back. 'Marko,' he said wonderingly. 'Prague, in—'

'Yes. Please, no more of it.' Her face had whitened. She went on steadily nevertheless. 'Whether this information will help I cannot judge. The facts are, however, that your government suspects a Russian involvement. Is this not so?'

Daintree said, 'Yes—and naturally so.'

'Then—as an initial premise—they are wrong.'

'They are?'

'Yes. I must not tell you how I know this, but I press upon you that it is fact. There has been no word from the Russian Embassy, no denial, because they wait until Moscow has been consulted in some detail. That consultation has now been made, but there is, as a result, a further involvement—or perhaps it is better called a complication.'

'Yes?'

'The denial will come, I think, tonight.'

'Then—'

She interrupted, looking into his eyes. 'It must not be believed—'

'But you've just said they're not involved!'

'*Were not involved in the beginning.*' She was leaning forward now, across the needlework screen. 'Now they are. If anybody is to get the three spies, it must be Moscow. Do you understand? In the circumstances, can your government not come to some accommodation with Moscow, Commander Daintree?'

* * *

Daintree was shown out by Esther Marko—still no contact with the M.P. As he crossed the hall, Daintree heard the booming tones of the Prime Minister coming from the drawing-room. He wondered if his tune would now undergo a change: decided, probably not. Frankly, Daintree was bemused and uncertain. It began to look as though there would be a race between the hijackers and the men from Moscow, but only after the event, presumably—the event that in fact would be a non-event if the hand-over was not made. Daintree grinned as he thought of the airborne hijackers under hot pursuit from Russian pirates. He went to his office and called the Commissioner: he too was still at work. Daintree took the lift up. He made a full report on Esther Marko.

The Commissioner asked, 'In that case, who the devil *is* behind the hijackers?'

'They could be on their own ... meaning, in effect, to flog Cunliffe, Delabier and Massey to Moscow afterwards.'

'Hardly on their own. Peking?'

Daintree shrugged, and grinned. 'You make it sound like a sort of big powers' spy auction!'

'Or some big international crime syndicate?'

'Could be, sir, could be.' Already Daintree had flipped some mental pages, but 'international crime' in the customary sense of the words was not quite his pigeon. 'Do we now use Interpol?'

'Not my decision, Commander.' The Commissioner puffed out his cheeks. 'If only we knew which airfield they have in mind!'

'That'll be notified shortly, sir. But *only* if we look like moving the prisoners.'

'You mean ... ?'

'Sir,' Daintree said with conviction, 'I mean this: we're going to get nowhere at all unless we seem to be moving the way they want. They're not going to stick their necks out otherwise. Unless we move, that coach stays hidden—and by God we've not had much joy out of the search yet! Unless we move, those hostages will die as surely as if we'd gunned them down ourselves.'

'So you're suggesting—once again—subterfuge?'

'I am.' Daintree added, 'In my view the Prime Minister's made a big mistake in appearing on television—'

'Did you see him?'

'No, sir, but I have a fair imagination.'

The Commissioner grinned. 'I don't suppose it led you too far astray—it did have all the appearance of a signed death-warrant.' He looked at his watch. 'I think we'll go and see Frazer-Petrie, both of us.'

* * *

Kahn, going back to the coach, said nothing to the passengers about the Prime Minister's evident determination: no point in making them reckless. He himself was relying on public clamour making itself felt. The Prime Minister had sounded almost too determined for his own good: there was going to be a strong reaction to pompous obstinacy. In Kahn's view, the Prime Minister had affronted the British sense of fair play, and never mind foul play from the other side. You didn't leave innocence to die the death, not in the last analysis. Kahn, staking all on ministerial love of power finally outweighing that pompous obstinacy, knew he was going to win.

Just after he got back, Lady Hanborough died. They all knew she was dead because of the sudden silence. All, that was, except her husband, who had fallen asleep. Kahn looked down at them, the living and the dead. The rest of them watched in a silence that no-one other than Kahn seemed wishful to break. Kahn bent and roughly shook Hanborough. 'Wake up, Your Lordship.'

The old man still slept. Kahn shook him again and shouted at him. He stirred. 'What's that?'

Kahn said, 'The old lady. Your wife.'

'Edie.' Hanborough started coughing. When he had finished he turned to his wife's body and said, 'She seems better. Her breathing...' He was delighted: tears, tears of old age and joy, sprang to his eyes. 'Edie, my dear.'

'Better nothing,' Kahn said in a voice of stone. 'She's dead, can't you see?'

'What was that?'

'*She's dead.* Come on now, she can't stay there, you old fool. Kerrigan, go and fetch some of the boys, there's work for them. Bring spades.' His voice echoed down the coach, smashed into the tenseness. Some of the women cried, upset by the latest tragedy, seeing this second death also as a foretaste that once again brought the future home with terrible clarity. Kerrigan left on his errand, clattering down the steps. Old Hanborough got to his feet, blindly, not knowing what he was about. Viciously, Kahn pushed him down again and he collapsed, weeping, on the floor, one hand groping up towards his wife. At the back, Rubery, relieving Silver, started along the gangway slowly, ready to assist Kahn in the event of trouble. Trouble seemed likely: Harkness was looking sick and mad. Trouble came, but not at first from Harkness. It came from the two youths with the transistor radios, now long silent in Kahn's possession. One of them, Peter Brewster, as Rubery came abreast of him, grabbed for Rubery's gun-arm. Getting a grip, he pulled Rubery down behind the cover of the seat-back in front of him, assisted now by his companion, Hurst. It was quickly done: Brewster smashed a knee into Rubery's face and felt the crunch of bone. Hurst took the gun, an automatic, stood up, and fired wildly towards Kahn. The bullet missed by a wide margin, richocheted off the metal handrail in front of Hanborough, and flew up into the roof. Then Harkness came in, flinging himself bodily at Kahn. Kahn took the impact, just rocking a little with Harkness clinging like a monkey to his back. Harkness got his hands round Kahn's throat, and squeezed. The coach was pandemonium: everywhere men and women got to their feet, disregarding danger now in the moment of triumph. Kahn was not using his gun: he was fighting for his life, his face darkening as the hands of Harkness tightened like steel. Sweat poured from Harkness, the sweat of concentrated endeavour to kill. Hanborough, his eyes blazing crazily, forgot the lifetime's teaching as to how an officer and a gentleman should behave towards a helpless enemy, got up and returned Kahn's back-hander blows across the face. It was, however, a short period of triumph only. From the rear of the coach someone, one of the women, cried out, *'They're coming!'*

The barn door had swung open and men were racing in. They were up the steps in an instant. One blow to the back of the head took Harkness off Kahn, who reeled back gasping for air. Frost, the large bald man, pushed heavily past Kahn.

The dim lighting glinted off dull grey metal, a wicked barrel, a drum. Frost stopped, eyes narrowed, watching. From behind a seat-back farther down, Rubery came out bottom first, dripping blood from his face as he emerged and stared at Frost.

Frost moved down the gangway and stopped with his sub-machine-gun aimed at Hurst and Brewster.

'Out,' he said.

'Look—'

'Out,' Frost said again. There was a dead silence, a total stillness. Brewster, the nearer of the two to Frost's gun-muzzle, looked around the coach, at the peering, fearful faces. Now, he read no help there: they were all thinking of themselves; they didn't want to get hurt. At the front end of the coach stood Kerrigan and one of the uniformed men, with guns aimed down the gangway, giving full cover. Harkness was lying on the floor, all doubled up. There would be no more heroics.

Brewster licked at his lips, eyes flickering, his young face like a jelly. He was nineteen years old, soon to start reading law at Cambridge: currently he was seeing too vividly the utter powerlessness of the law of England. His lips trembled.

'What are you going to do?' His voice was high, eyes pools of liquid.

Frost said, 'You'll see. Out. I won't tell you again. *Both* of you.'

Brewster moved out, followed by Hurst. The scared faces watched them along the gangway, down the steps, into the barn. In the barn were more men. Two of them used torches, bright and powerful. They kept the beams on Brewster and Hurst as they died, out in the barn, and the passengers saw it all, heard the sustained burst from Frost's gun, and saw the two bodies crumple into colandered heaps on the mucky straw.

That night, the burial parties were busy, their work taking them into the early hours of Sunday.

* * *

Sunday's dawn was bright and crisp, the good weather continuing. When the barn doors were swung back the passengers heard the sound of birdsong and saw a glimpse of freedom. Clean air swept in as the coach door was opened—a fresh breeze which blew into the barn and cleared away the night's terrible fug but not the memory of the night's worse events. Harkness, his face dead white with an unhealthy green tinge, was slumped in his seat behind the wheel, feeling sick and dizzy, knowing he was going to live—only to die a little later on. If they hadn't had a use for him, he would be dead already, like Brewster and Hurst. The blow on the head had left a crust of dried blood and a very painful ache. There was a singing in his ears and his sight was a trifle muzzy. Hanborough was asleep, although he was moaning softly, and his body was moving with a horrible restlessness. Sleep was the best thing for him. A woman in one of the middle seats was crying—one of the French women. Her friend was comforting her in a high and irritating monotone, the more irritating to Harkness because it was foreign. The Misses MacBean were being British, if such was not an insult to brave Scots lasses. They sat in a stiff silence, looking at nothing, their faces expressionless. But the foot of one of them, Miss Alison, the younger, in the gangway seat, was going tap-tap-tap against the supports of the seat ahead. Tap-tap-tap—the sound went on and on. Harkness had listened to this as well as to the French woman's monotony with jagging nerves. *Why the bloody hell didn't her elder sister shut her up?* Just when it was getting wholly unbearable, someone did, in a harsh torrent of effective sound: the German hausfrau, Borchardt.

'I beg your pardon,' Miss Alison said. 'I simply didn't realize....'

'Danke!' Frau Borchardt sat back again, like a huge cottage loaf with the beginning of a dark moustache. She breathed down her thick nose, hard, a kind of snort: the British were so emotional, so nervous of death. Frau Borchardt, whose youth had been spent in Hitler's Germany and in Hitler's war, was inured to a high degree to the inevitability of death. As she settled back, things began happening in the barn, events watched closely by Harkness. Wooden boxes, clearly very heavy, were being carried in and stowed in the boot, one after the other—an apparently endless succession, about enough, Harkness reckoned, to fill all 120 cubic feet of boot. The boxes had the look of explosives containers: Kahn had spoken of a 'big bang'. Room for the new consignment was made by the removal of the passengers' baggage, which was taken out to the barn. When the boxes had all been loaded, open cardboard cartons of food were brought in and also put in the boot. Harkness wondered about this. The deadline was now less than twenty-four hours away, yet they were being provisioned, by the look of it, to withstand something like a siege.

Hope flickered: was Kahn, perhaps, not quite so confident as he appeared? Or was he merely being prudent, willing to extend his deadline if need be, to accommodate the authorities? Only time would bring the answers, of course.... After the food came cans of diesel fuel to top up the tank. So they were going to move out: that much appeared deducible, at all events.

When the stowage was complete—and this included, for some reason, many cans of petrol—Kahn left the barn, shutting and barring the doors behind him. On guard in the coach, answering no questions from Harkness, were Kerrigan, Silver, Rubery and Frost; a double-banked watch taking no risks however cowed the passengers might be. Outside, a car started up, and the noise of its engine faded as it moved along the road to Balliemore. In the car was a tight-faced Kahn now within a stone's throw of his destiny: Kahn drove a long way that day, taking it fast across the belt of Scotland to Fort William in Argyll, driving down uncrowded roads through breathtaking scenery, through Aberfeldy, along the shores of Loch Tay, and into the Pass of Glencoe via Glen Dochart, crossing the sky-blue water of Loch Leven by the Ballachulish ferry. There were police around, and troops. Kahn was stopped and questioned. Had he seen a blue and gold coach belonging to South of England Motor Services? He was sorry but he had not—naturally, he would have reported anything, he'd read the papers, hadn't he? Kahn drove on, grinning at the helpless uniforms fading from view in wing mirrors. Now and again a helicopter passed over him, heading for the mountains or dropping into the glens. For a while the road was blocked by an armoured convoy—blocked till he was courteously waved past. He grinned again. Stupid bastards! From Fort William Kahn made another of his telephone calls to London.

'All as planned. Stage, Liftout Three. Okay?'

"Okay.'

'In position 01.30 hours. Will transmit when in station. Is Skyferry okay?'

'Ready and waiting.'

Kahn nodded satisfaction into the mouthpiece. 'Right, fine. No contact before 18.00 hours tonight. That's all.'

He rang off and beat it out of the call-box. He faded towards his car, parked the other end of the town. Once on the move, he heard the police cars. He grinned: the stupid bastards had a degree of efficiency but they weren't fast enough.... Kahn drove out of Fort William, taking a different route home, past Loch Laggan, heading for the intersection with the A9 north of Pitlochry. A nice day for a drive...

10

FRAZER-PETRIE, Daintree thought very early on the Sunday morning, wasn't square: he was cubed, set into amber, pickled solid. The Civil Service mind... Daintree felt sick. The Soviet Embassy had run the British Civil Service a close second: flat denial and, thereafter, closed lips. Even the others —American, West German, French, the supposed refuges of their nationals—they didn't want to be pressed too hard for help. Terrorists, they all seemed to suggest, though they didn't say it outright, were better left alone: a display of masterly inactivity was the only defence for diplomats. But Frazer-Petrie was Britain's personal problem: nothing would move the man—nothing.

They had tried it all.

'For God's sake... not much more than eighteen hours to go—'

'We're doing all we can. Police, armed forces—'

The Commissioner banged the table. 'Tell me something I *don't* know! It's not enough. Can't you put yourself in the place of those men and women, just for a moment?'

'I know it's... diabolical. But you heard the Prime Minister.'

'I did.' This was said hollowly, with scorn. 'Is he quite impervious?'

Frazer-Petrie lifted an eyebrow. 'Impervious? I can't say. But he *is* determined. I—'

'Now look.' The Commissioner leaned across the shine of mahogany and waved a finger in Frazer-Petrie's offended face. 'I'm not asking—necessarily—for Cunliffe, Delabier and Massey to be handed over—'

'My dear chap, if you *did*—'

'Though I'm not sure I shouldn't, on humanitarian grounds,

and rather than see those people blown up, or shot in cold blood, I'd be inclined to let our spies run with my blessing when the crunch comes. But I'm not asking that.' The Commissioner wiped sweat from his face with a linen handkerchief. 'I'm only asking for a straw to be put into the wind. That's all. Let it be known we'll talk.'

Frazer-Petrie said, 'But that's *not* quite all, in fact, is it?'

'Not quite,' the Commissioner admitted. 'There's the question of movement—the question of subterfuge, and it *is* only that.'

'It's no use,' Frazer-Petrie said. 'The P.M. simply won't look at it. I'm sorry, but I really can't say any more than that. It's not in my hands, you know.' He took up a telephone that had buzzed at him and spoke into it. 'Yes? Yes. . . .' He looked up at Sir Richard Smith. 'Just one moment, Commissioner, it's the P.M. coming on.' He waited; they all waited. Daintree felt strongly that there was something of import coming through to Frazer-Petrie. Frazer-Petrie's conversation was unrevealing, monosyllabic: yes sir and no sir, respectfully, in a muted voice. Daintree shook with impatience: time was so cruelly short! He looked out of the window into the fresh green of a garden, only London-fresh with a patina of tiredness and traffic fumes, but still green and with life in it. Like those people in the coach, Daintree thought, living a half-life under constant threat. The voice of the Prime Minister rattled through from Frazer-Petrie's telephone, loud, hectoring, authoritative. At last Frazer-Petrie rang off, with a touch of obsequiousness like the colonel who was said to salute the telephone each time his general rang. Frazer-Petrie's aristocratic face was pink and uncomfortable.

'Well, well,' he said, sounding petulant.

'What is it?' the Commissioner rapped.

'A change of mind, Commissioner... I'm to inform the Home Secretary, but I think I can tell you now. You'll be pleased to hear it.' Frazer-Petrie stared away across the top of the Commissioner's head. 'It's to be leaked that we might concede, though in fact, of course, we won't. Cunliffe, Delabier and Massey are to be moved together to army detention quarters in Colchester, handy for airfields in East Anglia, under the orders and control of the military authority.'

The Commissioner let out a long breath. He said, 'Thank God! Let us pray that it's not too late.'

Outside in the car that took them back to the Yard, he said, 'Frankly I expected that, Daintree. The Sunday papers... he's had a shocking press today!'

Daintree nodded. Today he was glad enough to note the power of the press, to note the changed attitude of the British public which on this occasion coincided with his own views. Once, back in the fifties say, they would have been in an indignant mood about any threat, turning their vitriol and their cartoons upon the common enemy: now, indignation was reserved for their own side for its lack of humanity towards helpless people. The concept of loyalty to the State was no longer emotion-rousing and had not been for many years: a threat to Britain was, sadly, no longer seen as a threat to the individual.... Daintree checked himself: he was mentally arguing against his own case. In any event, there was still not to be, in fact, a handover, a surrender. His job was still to ensure that Cunliffe, Delabier and Massey remained in Britain. To that end, he would now have to liaise very closely with the army authorities, a prospect he didn't entirely relish.

At the Yard, a report had come in from Scotland: no leads to the coach, but a possible lead to where it had recently rested. Up that track, that forest ride on Deeside where the imprint of a heavy vehicle had been noted, a little way from the clearing with the new-cut branches, a shallow grave had been detected and investigated. The body of a young man had been found. Death from shooting not more than five days ago according to forensic. There was no identification on the body but enquiries were proceeding. Daintree wasn't happy: the hijackers having once killed—and in his view they were undoubtedly the culprits—they had no reason left not to kill again. In the meantime there was work to be done and Daintree, leaving the Yard once more, drove to Whitehall and the Ministry of Defence. Here he conferred with a civil servant and a major-general, plus staff. He was given his orders, and was asked—somewhat perfunctorily, he thought—for his views. Cunliffe, Delabier and Massey, he was told, would be moved by troops of the Household Division to Colchester from Pentonville, to which prison the three of them would be temporarily returned by the civil power as soon as possible.

* * *

Soon after 17.00 hours, Kahn was back in the barn from his drive to Fort William's telephone facilities. Calling Rubery from the coach, he went into a huddle in the farmhouse, together with Frost and the police-uniformed men from Glasgow. After this Kerrigan and Silver were replaced in the coach by other men and reported for their briefing. Kahn was confident still: he, as well as the Prime Minister, the Commissioner of Metropolitan Police and Daintree, had read the Sunday papers. The government was unpopular, the Prime Minister personally the prime target of attack. There had been interviews with some of the relatives—very nicely chosen, at any rate by some sections of the Sunday press: Jilly Ruff's parents, Susan Larcombe's parents who still did not know that their daughter was already a widow; many other likely tear-jerkers including the wife and children of the driver. Sons and daughters anxious about elderly mothers and fathers were contacted. There was a near-hysterical interview, conducted by transatlantic telephone, with the two younger daughters of the MacFees in Maine. The son of the blind man with the white stick was interviewed too, as was the younger brother of old Hanborough, who insisted that if Hanborough had said the hijackers meant to carry out their threat, then carry it out they would. His brother, he said emphatically, was not the sort of man to bend under a threat or tell a falsehood. Some of these interviews were also shown on the television news broadcasts; that of Hanborough's brother was immensely effective, and greatly pleased Kahn.

At 18.15 Kahn went back to the coach and stood near Harkness with his gun inevitably pointing down the gangway. He said, 'It won't be long now, ladies and gentlemen.' He looked at his watch. 'I don't suppose I need remind you, the deadline is a little under eight hours off. Soon after that, you may be free. So don't be foolish at the last, all right? No tricks. You've seen what happens to people who try to be funny—that can and will happen again if necessary. In the meantime, we have some roadwork to do—we have a rendezvous to reach. We move out from here at midnight, not a long drive. As usual, driver Harkness will be behind the wheel.' He looked sideways at Harkness. 'The moment he tries anything, he dies. All right, Mr Harkness?'

Harkness nodded, saying nothing. He felt sick inside, and was still rocky from that blow on the head. Dumbly miserable, he felt he had let his passengers down with a thump, he should have done something, anything... *but what?* As to that, a time still might come—might! He bowed his head over his steering-wheel and put his hands up to cover his tears, thinking of Mary and the children, wondering what they would be feeling now, what they would be doing. Teatime on Sunday was normally a happy time except that it meant the week-end was nearly over and there was school next day. But today! There would be no sleep tonight in the small, neat Peckham home, and no school tomorrow.

Kahn, his statement of intent delivered, again left the coach. The watch was maintained by Rubery, Kerrigan, and one of Rubery's men.

* * *

A little before Kahn's pep-talk—at 18.00 hours precisely—a call by telephone had reached the Home Office. The hoarse and faintly accented voice of a man had made one simple statement, very concise: 'Rendezvous for hand-over at 02.00 hours tomorrow morning will be RAF Hatherleigh.' Then the line clicked off. The message was passed at once to all concerned authorities; Prime Minister, Home Secretary, Scotland Yard, Defence Ministry, Edinburgh police. From these authorities it was passed on to Commander Household Division, Daintree, police forces in East Anglia and the officer in command at Colchester. At 09.00 hours that morning, Cunliffe, Delabier and Massey had begun their move to Pentonville Prison from Albany, Durham and Dartmoor respectively, in strong police convoys that had blasted all road users out of their paths with screaming sirens and flashing blue lights. Cunliffe, Delabier and Massey had travelled in black Jaguars each with three armed guards. Each Jaguar was escorted by two patrol cars and two police Range Rovers ahead, and the same again in rear. There were also six outriders plus two more well behind as a long-stop. The A3 from Portsmouth, the A30 from Exeter, and the M1, had seldom seen comparable speeds. At Pentonville the army had taken over all three spies. Still in their separate Jaguars but now with guarding redcaps, Cunliffe, Delabier and Massey had been sped to Colchester with escorting Land Rovers wearing the insignia and guidons of the Household Cavalry of the Royal Armoured Corps. Ahead and astern were weapons-carriers and personnel-carriers filled with armed troops. A solitary police car was in the lead to clear the roads for the passage of the vital convoy. Into the Sunday-evening quiet of Colchester's streets they had brought sudden drama. A small crowd watched the vehicles pass swiftly through guarded gates into a military barracks; and once they were in the usual guard was trebled, and a strong perimeter patrol with guard dogs and sub-machine-guns was established. With that convoy into the Army's domain went Daintree, riding with the major in command. Daintree insisted on seeing the prisoners locked up, personally. He approved the arrangements: the guard was heavy by any standard. At 18.20 the message from the Home Office reached Colchester from two sources: the Defence Ministry and the Commissioner. Daintree spoke to the Commissioner on the telephone.

'Hatherleigh,' he repeated. 'Cambridgeshire, under the county re-organization... near St Ives?'

'Right. Ex-RAF—still owned by the Ministry, but not used. I'm told the runways are in a poor condition, but probably just viable for these people's purposes.'

'What are the orders, sir?'

'I don't know yet. You'll have to hang on, Daintree—'

'The Prime Minister?'

'Yes. He's havering now the crunch is coming; can't make up his mind.'

'That's unlike him, isn't it?'

There was a pause. 'Yes. Not that I can't appreciate the risks, the weight of the decision.' Another pause. 'We just may have to help him out, Daintree.'

Daintree stiffened, felt a curious thrill, a sense of extreme danger. 'I beg your pardon?'

'I haven't said a thing,' the Commissioner told him, 'but I'll back anything you decide to do. I think you understand. I have the fullest confidence in your judgment, you know that.'

Daintree said, 'Thank you, sir. I'll be doing my best. Just one thing: I'd like a clarification as to the division of responsibility... as between me and the Army command?'

The voice rattled in his ear: 'You know it already, Daintree!'

'A re-statement, sir... in view of—what you've just said.'

'Ah—yes.' The Commissioner cleared his throat. 'The civil power runs this country, Daintree, not the Army—we're not Greeks. The Army's part ends when our spies leave Colchester ... do you get me? And that decision's ours—yours, now. If necessary, you can invoke Security. I won't be more specific. Anything else?'

'Nothing else, sir.'

'Then the best of luck to you.' The Commissioner rang off. Daintree sat for a moment in thought, alone in the colonel's office. This was being handed to him on a gold plate: the Commissioner's meaning had been fairly obvious. If he should decide to move Cunliffe, Delabier and Massey closer to the rendezvous—strictly for propaganda purposes, of course, still no genuine hand-over—then he could do it without letting Whitehall know. And the savage clamp of Security would drop with its heavy weight on the Colchester military command.

Daintree got to his feet. Making his way to the Officers' Mess, he sweated a little. The responsibility bordered on the awesome.

* * *

The Prime Minister made his decision at 21.30 hours: there was positively—he repeated this firmly—to be no hand-over, no surrendering to impudent threat. Neither were Cunliffe, Delabier and Massey to be moved closer to Hatherleigh—they would remain under firm guard in Colchester. He had done the most he could to go along with Daintree's ideas and he could concede nothing more. The national consideration must now come first: he refrained from putting it into words that the victims must now face sacrifice. But he gave orders that troops were to be sent at once to the vicinity of the old RAF airfield at Hatherleigh, under a heavy security cloak, and to conceal themselves to await touchdown of some as yet unknown aircraft belonging to the people behind the hijack. This aircraft was to be surrounded and its crew held prisoner. The boot, the Prime Minister said with a sure confidence that equalled Kahn's, would then be on the other foot.

When this decision reached him, Daintree blew up. He said, 'God damn it, Colonel, the moment anyone touches that aircraft, the coach passengers have had it! That's the whole nub of the thing... doesn't he *see* that?' He lifted his hands high. 'No doubt he thinks he's being so bloody clever...'

'Give him his due,' the soldier said, 'perhaps he is.'

Daintree stared. 'How, for God's sake?'

'If we take the flying crew, we can use them as a counter-threat to save the coach passengers... can't we?'

Daintree snapped, 'No. With all respect, you don't know hijackers. Nor does the Prime Minister. *I do!* They're fanatics, and they stick together—that's how they succeed. The flying crew will die rather than compromise the bastards in the coach, and the bastards in the coach'll never let the side down by quitting. They each know implicitly they can rely on the other. And quite apart from that, can you see us shooting down that flying crew, in cold blood, after an interval for parley? Because, frankly, I can't. So it'll be an empty threat, and known as such.'

The colonel said, 'Well, we've had our orders, Commander. We have to carry them out.'

'But you'll kill the coach passengers!'

The answer was stiffly formal: 'I'm sorry, but orders are orders.'

* * *

At 23.30 hours Harkness was ordered by Kahn to run his engine for test. With the barn doors open a little way and all lights off except for his instrument panel, he did so. It ran sweetly enough after a moment. Harkness could see no way of pulling the wool over Kahn's eyes enginewise just at this moment of starting up. Kahn, listening to the engine sounds, seemed satisfied.

'Okay,' he said. 'Switch off.'

Harkness switched off. Looking back along the gangway he saw the fresh tension in the faces of his passengers as they braced themselves for the final run. A mixture of emotions showed: there would be a degree of relief in the act of movement itself, of getting away from the barn's claustrophobia, back into the world. But the basic fear could now almost be felt as a physical force, an emanation of dread of what was soon to come. The only one now to appear unruffled was the blind man, John Pratt, who just sat and stared at nothing, very upright, with his white stick held between his legs and his clasped hands resting on the handle. His wife was sniffing, crying into a handkerchief—more concerned, Harkness felt sure, for herself than for her husband. So much younger... so many more years ahead. The two old ladies in black were red with crying now, and sat holding each other's hands tight while their mouths munched at spittle. Hanborough, sitting by himself, seemed oblivious, did not seem to care any more now that Edie was gone. He'd probably welcome death now, Harkness thought, and didn't blame him. His face had a white, papery look with a yellow tinge and a kind of transparency behind it. Kahn got down: Harkness watched him moving with his torch past the windows, then heard the boot being opened up. Kahn would be checking... the hand of Harkness moved almost without an act of will towards the key in the ignition. A dash out now, minus Kahn, a smash-run through the barn's half-open doors? But what, with Kerrigan and Silver embarked with guns, could that achieve? Answer: obvious! Harkness gave a sigh, and let his hand fall on his knee. Behind, Kahn was indeed checking—just to set his mind at rest before the last leg. A nasty mixture—petrol and high explosive. Kahn checked the cartons of food, the contents of which were going to pick up the petrol smell, and the cans of water. He checked reeled lengths of fuse and reels of barbed wire brought in from the farmhouse. All okay.

Kahn went back to the front, took the keys from Harkness, returned and locked the boot. As he did so, the final stocks were brought into the coach and stowed beneath the rear seats; sub-machine-guns and drums of ammunition, rifles of the newest military pattern, hand-grenades. Next came a re-shuffle of the passengers, just a small one: Hanborough was joined by a short fat man named Harris, a purple-faced man with heavy jowls and a nervous manner. He and Hanborough were put in seats farther down the coach; Mrs Harris was re-seated with Ernie Peach whose wife was still tending Susan Larcombe; the McFees were shifted back to where Peter Brewster and his friend Hurst had sat. When this redistribution was complete, other men embarked: Rubery, still in police uniform, with four more men also dressed as policemen. Rubery, now wearing a sergeant's stripes, sat where the Hanboroughs had sat; two of the others sat behind Harkness, displacing Kahn and Kerrigan to the seats next behind. The remaining two went to the rear, sitting with Silver over the cache of arms. A minute later, the flash of a torch came from the road.

Ahead of the coach, the two police cars started up, their engines sounding loud in the barn, a smell of exhaust sweeping back. Kahn nodded at Harkness. 'Start up.'

Harkness, feeling a prickle along his spine, did so. 'Move?' he asked.

'No, hold it, just do what I say, that's all.'

Harkness waited. Within seconds, another brief flash came. Kahn said, 'Okay, we'll go.'

Harkness moved, coming out behind the police-cars, out of the barn and across the farmyard towards the gate. The big man, Frost, standing by the gate with a companion, waved. 'Go right,' Kahn said. Harkness brought the coach round, into the road.

'Stop.'

He stopped. The rearmost police car backed past him, and took up station behind. 'Move,' Kahn said. He was still standing, right by Harkness, as ready as ever with his gun. 'Put on your lights.' Harkness flicked a switch, the road lit like day under dipped headlights. Ahead and astern, the police also put on lights, and the blue lamps began their flashing. Kahn ordered all overhead lights to be put on inside the coach; then he sat down, with Kerrigan, behind the uniformed coppers. He called to Harkness. 'Just follow the car ahead. He'll flick for the turns.'

'Where are we going?' Harkness asked.

There was a laugh. 'You'll see! Just shut up—and drive.'

11

TROOPS left Colchester—no airlift, but a fast road convoy up into Cambridgeshire, not all that far to go. Infantry, with a company of the Royal Greenjackets, the army's marksmen. A detachment of the Royal Air Force Regiment was already being deployed from RAF Wyton, where aircraft were standing by for further orders. Daintree, watching the road convoy leave Colchester, felt the reaction in his stomach. Those poor bloody hostages, wherever they were . . . as good as dead now. Yet there was some consolation in the undoubted fact that the hijackers would be expecting some troop movement like this, or at the very least would be taking it into account: thus, there might even now be hope that the situation was not worsened. Alongside that thought came another: confidence, on the part of the hijackers, was still supremely high. They must obviously realize, for one thing, the proximity of RAF Wyton to the old airfield at Hatherleigh.

Daintree, before the troops left Colchester, had rung the Yard: the Commissioner was not there, he was at the Home Office. Daintree rang the Home Office: the Commissioner had just left. By the time Daintree finally got him, the troop movement was under way. Daintree, who was on a closed line, was almost frantically rude about events.

'All right, all right,' the Commissioner snapped at him. 'Points taken—all of them! But it's a cabinet decision and there's damn-all *I* can do. Hang on to your temper, Daintree.'

'*Is* it a cabinet decision? Or is it—'

'No comment. I'm a public servant, so are you. Like the Army, we obey orders—if not quite so blindly and rigidly. Get me, Daintree?'

Daintree paused. 'What you said earlier, sir?'

'It still stands. In the last resort—on the spot—the civil power will have the last word. That's all, Daintree.' The Commissioner had then rung off abruptly. Daintree, standing alone at the window of the colonel's office while his host saw his troops away, made up his mind to take a big risk. The very thought made him sweat, but deep down inside he believed—he *knew*—it to be the only way left. When the colonel came back, this time in company with a major-general who seemed to have materialized from nowhere, Daintree stated a firm intention.

He said, 'I'm taking over Cunliffe, Delabier and Massey. I'm taking them over, back into police custody, and I'm moving them out.'

The officers stared, looking outraged. 'You can't do that,' the major-general said.

'I can, General, and I'm going to. I'm sorry. This is no reflection on Army security, of course.' Daintree stood his ground, firm as a rock. 'I have my reasons, police reasons.'

'Where d'you propose moving them, may I ask?'

Daintree hesitated. 'I shall tell you that, General, though I'm not obliged to. I'm taking them . . . closer to the airfield at Hatherleigh. Just in case they can be used—'

'Handed over?'

'No. Used for bargaining perhaps. I say perhaps . . . we have to play this by ear, General.' Daintree was sweating more than ever. 'I'm personally convinced we must play along to the limit, or those hostages are going to die. This is no time—with respect—to leave matters to troops. Your troops are on the way there and there's nothing I can do about that now, but I must insist on making . . . my own plans. I—'

'It'll have to be referred to the Ministry, you realize that?'

'No, sir.' Daintree shook his head, standing four-square to the brass and the red tabs. 'That'll not be necessary, nor desirable—'

'What's that?'

'Nor desirable,' Daintree repeated with emphasis. 'I have to ask you to maintain the strictest security as of now.' He looked, ostentatiously, at his watch. 'There is little time to go—'

'But damn it all, man!' The major-general's face was a study in incredulity, truculence, and accusation of God knew what. 'Security... the Defence Ministry... *damn it, they're synonymous!*'

'But telephones are not. Even closed lines, General. Believe me, I know what I'm doing. I happen to be a senior officer of the Special Branch, with very special knowledge and somewhat over-riding powers... I'm sorry to put it that way. But I know you understand, General. From now on out, I have to insist that any communication with the Defence Ministry or any other authority must be in person and not by telephone.' In-person reports took time: Daintree stared at the major-general, who exchanged looks with the colonel. Decision was on a tightrope: but the Special Branch carried weight and all present knew that. The major-general gave a throat-clearing cough, tugged at his collar, swiped at khaki thighs with a silver-topped cane. That was when Daintree, almost sighing with relief, knew he had won. Gladly enough he agreed that the responsibility was his, and his alone. He would give his discharge on that. This important point sorted out, he was driven with the major-general to speak with the Chief Constable. Here there was more argument but the matter was finally settled. Within ninety minutes of the troop convoy's departure, Cunliffe, Delabier and Massey were back on the road and heading north-west towards the Hatherleigh tarmac in cars stiff with police and escorted by police Range Rovers and outriders. Daintree, in the rearmost Range Rover, sagged with reaction: he didn't feel unappreciative of the Army, but he was happier with his own kind. The night drive along traffic-free roads was mainly fast: the occasional juggernaut, trundling from the south-eastern ports, caused the odd delay, but not much: the scream of police sirens achieved the desired effect. Daintree halted the cars and the escort when they were around half a mile from Hatherleigh, a little north of the runway where there was good cover from trees, got down and walked along the line, checking, assuring himself of what he knew must be the case: that all was well. He looked in at the three spies in their three separate cars. Their faces were now full of strain, of uncertainty mixed with anticipation of possible freedom. Daintree scowled back at them. Freedom for spies he found detestable, but still wondered how he was going to act at the final curtain. He was, by training, by experience, a policeman: policemen didn't let villains go. And to let them go would finish his career—he was not, could not be, unaware of that. He must watch his emotions that night, more carefully than ever before in his life.

He turned his back on the cars, looked around at the night-quiet countryside, the fringes of fenland, dark, mysterious, remote—a good choice of airlift rendezvous was this, with a clear run in and out again over the east coast. Daintree looked up at the sky; a lot of heavy cloud, spasmodic moonlight breaking to silver the fields, the dykes, the clumps of trees, the few hedges. He could hear the isolated cries of night birds and the occasional scurry of a small land animal making homeward, or going out on an affray for food. Daintree walked back along the road, his feet crunching on a gritty surface of loose chippings. He stopped by his Range Rover, his mobile command post for the night.

'Wireless okay?'

'All okay, sir.'

Daintree nodded at the Chief Inspector from Colchester. He didn't want to chivvy, to be a tiresome senior officer, forever checking and being a bloody nuisance, but tonight his nerves were on the brink. That, he thought, probably applied to all present. A lot of people thought the police were not human, but they made a mistake in thinking that. Those hostages had become almost blood relations, this was nearly a family matter now...

Daintree looked again at the sky as he shivered slightly in cold, damp night air. He was certain the aircraft would come in from easterly, from across the North Sea, and would be tracked in by the radar stations of the air defence network, the thing Cunliffe, Delabier and Massey had tried their best to blow. Again, this was something that the hijackers would expect—again, they would not be worried by the fact. Why should they be? Daintree reflected, bitterly, that always hijackers held the best cards, *all* the bloody cards... Looking at his watch for the hundredth time, he saw that it was now seven minutes past midnight: Monday was upon them.

* * *

In London—in Whitehall, in Downing Street—there was mounting tension. The Prime Minister waited, his face full of angry concern for many aspects, handy for several telephones and attended by his private secretary and by Frazer-Petrie, plus a high official from the Home Office. In the Home Office, the Home Secretary himself was at instant readiness to take decisions. In the Defence Ministry the Chief of the General Staff waited in a nail-biting mood with the Chief of Air Staff. In New Scotland Yard, the Commissioner of Metropolitan Police stared down from his high window, keeping his fingers crossed for Commander Daintree and his personal tightrope. The news had come by report in person of a Staff Colonel from Colchester; just a few minutes ago it had reached Scotland Yard. Daintree was out on a limb now: so was the Commissioner, Daintree's backer. The Prime Minister was said to be furious but under control: at this stage he knew he had to leave it to the trained experts. But failure would lead inevitably to a massive head-rolling...

Shrill and urgent, a telephone rang. A Chief Superintendent reached for it, but the Commissioner beat him to it. 'Yes?'

'One unidentified aircraft, sir, reported crossing the coast inwards above Cromer, heading 223 degrees. This report is timed at 00.34 hours and comes from Defence Ministry.'

'Thank you.' The Commissioner put down the handset carefully, then looked up at the Chief Superintendent. 'They're in,' he said. 'Daintree should be picking them up any moment now.'

* * *

From Balliemore, with the stern of his coach down heavily because of the load of explosive, Harkness had followed the tail lights and blue flash of the leading police car along the B846 through Dalriach and Tummel Bridge, along the B8019 to the intersection with the A9 John o'Groats to Edinburgh road at Ballinluig in Perthshire. Here he had followed the right-hand turn of the leading police car and headed on down towards Perth. There was little traffic around apart from heavy stuff hauling loads through the night: as in the case of Daintree's East Anglian drive, Rubery's police cars blasted the lorries into giving free passage. The coach and its escort came down fast through sleeping Pitlochry, through Dunkeld, through wooded country, past long drops to their right from time to time, headlamps beaming out over nothingness on the bends. They passed genuine police patrols still carrying out the search, as the deadline drew close for Tour Eighteen. They swept past them, saw the stares, the curious faces, the interest in the police escort and the uniformed constables inside the coach behind the driver and at the back. Rubery, in his sergeant's uniform, was now standing in the front, facing the back, steadying himself on the handrail before the front nearside seat: he had a guarding look, which was both real and propagandist. In Pitlochry and in Dunkeld, and later in Perth, where the speed was slowed, they passed coppers on the beat, on foot and in Pandas: there was no reason for them to be stopped, and they were not. Nevertheless, as Harkness followed his leader on to the A90 from Perth southwards, a report was made to police headquarters in Edinburgh, a report for information only. As a result of this report, the leading police car was waved down between Bridge of Earn and Bein Inn.

Obediently its driver pulled in and was approached by a police motor-cyclist. After a short conversation, the crash-helmeted constable came over to Harkness. Rubery leaned across Harkness, looming danger to life. 'What's the idea?' he asked. 'We're in a hurry.'

The constable jerked a hand towards the car ahead. 'They say you've got the hijackers, Sergeant.' He banged the side of the coach. 'Wrong colour, isn't it?'

'Yes. Camouflage. We've got them, all right!'

'Well . . . congratulations! And thank God too.' The constable smiled, a happy man 'Have you reported, Sergeant?'

'No. Both radios gone—there was a bit of a tussle. I didn't stop in Perth, and I don't want to stop now. I'm taking them to Edinburgh direct. All right?'

'All right, Sergeant. I'll report in for you.'

Rubery gave a big smile. 'Do that—and thanks.'

'Want any help—outrider?'

'No, we can manage. Just make your report, laddie, that's all. And good-night to you.'

'Good-night...' The constable walked away towards his motor-cycle and they got moving again. The constable gave them a cheery wave, and they saw him talking into his transmitter. Harkness felt sick in the guts again, sick with himself —but what would have been the use in getting the motor-cyclist killed? He glanced in his mirror at Kahn. Kahn was grinning, giving the fake sergeant a thumbs-up, well done. Kahn was still not worried: journey's end must be very, very near now, but still there had been no clues. Driving on, Harkness wondered: what could the idea be now? Where were they heading—right down into England, all the way to this East Anglian airfield mentioned in that first news broadcast in the early stages of the hijack? But for Christ's sake... they'd be rumbled long before that, surely, now that genuine policeman had put in his report, and then they failed to show up in Edinburgh? And they couldn't be heading—not now—for Edinburgh, could they? If the goal was England, they would presumably keep well clear of Edinburgh and go in south from say, Stirling, down the A80, branching off to head through Moffat and Lockerbie for Carlisle... and then where?

* * *

The report from the police motor-cyclist was passed on a wave of euphoria from Edinburgh to the Home Office in London, and from there to, among others, New Scotland Yard. The Commissioner took the call himself, stood amazed, incredulous, happy. He almost danced.

'They've got it—the Scottish police! They've got the coach!'

The Chief Superintendent mopped his streaming face. 'Thank God! The passengers?'

'Apparently unharmed—at least, that's the assumption. The report was sketchy, says Edinburgh. A young constable, somewhat overwhelmed they fancy.' He gave the Chief Superintendent the facts as known. 'They should be in Edinburgh soon. Then we'll know.'

'It's a bloody miracle,' the Chief Superintendent said in a shaking voice. 'A bloody deliverance ... at the eleventh hour, to coin a phrase!' He paused. 'Stand down now, sir?'

'No. There's many a slip ... the coach has some way to go, to Edinburgh. We'll play safe till the next word comes through, I think.'

* * *

Confoundment awaited the tentative speculations of Harkness: at Kinross the leading car was still on the A90 for Edinburgh. Still Kahn was saying nothing, but the rear-view mirror showed suddenly increased tension in his face as he told Harkness to flash his headlights twice. When Harkness did this, the car ahead increased speed. So, to orders, did Harkness. They belted along, swaying. Down through Cowdenbeath, into the Kingdom of Fife. Through Crossgates. Soon, below the road to the left, the lights of Inverkeithing came in view, close now to the Firth of Forth. Down on the A92 from Inverkeithing were a number of heavy vehicles, waiting: Harkness saw them move for the approach road leading to the A90 and the bridge. They joined the A90 behind the coach, keeping a fair distance. The convoy, lights flashing between high, rocky banks, slowed as genuine police were seen ahead, in a pool of light where the road ran on to the bridge. They were waved down. Harkness, his stomach loose as water, felt the presence of too many concealed guns, too close. Yet something told him this was his moment, the last he could expect, at any rate until they met the sealed border into England. He stopped the coach behind the leading car and watched the approach of a bevy of policemen under an inspector who spoke to him through the window.

'You're the hijack party?'

Harkness nodded, noting that the police officer was armed. That fact gave him the impetus to speak. In a hoarse, high voice he said, 'Yes, we are, and we're still ...' His voice trailed away: his vocal cords seemed inhibited, inhibited by the pressure in his side of Kahn's gun. Kahn had got to his feet, and was now leaning across Harkness. Smiling, he addressed the inspector.

'Excuse me,' he said.

The police officer looked up, right into Kahn's eyes. 'Yes?'

'Just this.' Kahn was still smiling when suddenly he brought up his gun and fired right into the inspector's face. Harkness saw surprise, a spread of blood that became a red mask, then a gush through powder-blackened teeth. The inspector fell to the ground. In the hush, the hush of utter appalled bewilderment that followed, Kahn dug his gun hard into Harkness. At the same time he flicked the headlights. As the fake police car ahead started up and moved towards the bridge carriageway, keeping in the left-hand lane, Kahn snapped, 'Drive for your life, Harkness. Lead us in, past the cop car. Foot down hard—*go!*'

Harkness did as he was told. He gathered speed, seemed to hurtle on to the bridge. Behind came both the police cars. There was more firing and in his rear-view mirror Harkness saw the battle: the heavy vehicles from the A92 were closing in behind, following the coach on to the bridge, and spurts of flame were coming from what seemed to be sub-machine-guns, bullets smashing into the police. Driving on fast, coming up the rise of the span, Harkness saw the dark waters of the Forth, glinting in moonlight, and high above, the ghostly outlines of the heavy cables and their huge, heavenward-reaching, steel supports. From ahead, more sounds and sights of battle; then the lights of other vehicles moving north—moving towards them in their own lane, against the thin traffic flow. Rocking dangerously past slower southbound cars, ordinary bridge users who had joined the bridge before the trouble had started, Harkness saw the faces peering up from them, scared faces, faces of men who had heard the firing. His hands shook on the wheel. Kahn, as they came to a central position on the great bridge, spoke again.

'Stop, Harkness.'

'What?'

'*Stop!*'

Sweating, shaking, Harkness obeyed. Looking automatically

in his driving mirror he saw strange cars, a Cortina, a Bentley, a Bedford dormobile—more innocents trapped between the coach and the heavy vehicles behind. There was an odd silence, a terrible silence. Kahn broke it. He said, 'Journey's end, ladies and gentlemen. Here we stay. Silver?'

'Yes?'

'Run out the fuses.'

Silver moved up the gangway, gun in hand, watchful. From behind, Harkness heard the heavy vehicles from Inverkeithing braking squeakily to a stop, saw in his mirror men getting out of the trapped cars, looking around fearfully, not yet understanding exactly what they had become involved in. Ahead the northbound vehicles, as heavy as those behind, also stopped, closing the trap. Silver got down with the boot keys and moved astern. Rubery's uniformed men moved towards the trapped cars. Silver began ferreting in the boot. In a tense silence again, the passengers listened to dragging sounds, clinking sounds, metallic noises. Harkness sucked in breath: the future was clear enough now. If and when the big explosion came, Kahn meant to blow up the bridge as well as themselves. Harkness had no knowledge of explosives or of their effect, but the quantity embarked had seemed to him big: at the very least, surely, the detonation would tear a great gap in the carriageways, even bring down the great steel cables and support towers—weaken the whole support structure of a massive and inspiring engineering feat. The sounds from Silver continued. From the cars behind—the Cortina, the Bentley, the Bedford dormobile—came the sounds of raised voices, high, scared as apparent police behaved in an unpolicemanlike manner.

Far below them, the river glinted with a touch of evil, of menace.

12

BEFORE the aircraft had come in, Daintree had detached himself and his command vehicle and had gone on the prowl, looking for the troops. After a longish search he found the officer in charge, a major, crouched in a ditch with a platoon of infantry, and he crouched with him, uncomfortably.

'Where's the rest?' he asked, keeping his voice low.

'Spread around the perimeter.'

'Their orders?'

'To remain in cover and not show themselves.'

'Until when, Major?'

'Until I say.'

'How do you say?'

The major indicated his attendant signaller. 'Walkie-talkie.'

Daintree grunted. There was no moon just now, it had sailed away behind the heavy cloud: the soldiers were mere blobs of greater darkness than the night itself. The Army vehicles, like his own, were covered by clumps of trees. It was very quiet. The men were like ghosts, making no sound at all. So far, the major said, no-one had been seen on the airfield, or near it.

'There won't be anyone,' Daintree said, 'not till the aircraft comes in. And then only from the plane itself.'

'I'd not like to come in without a flare-path...'

'Nor me,' Daintree said. 'But it's been done before, back in the war.'

'True.'

There was a faint stir of wind that gently rippled the grass along the lip of the ditch. While driving in, closer to the old airfield than he had been whilst with his convoy, Daintree had looked across at the runways. For a time there had been moon enough to see clearly: cracked and broken concrete with scrubby bushes growing here and there, derelict hangars and stores with caved-in roofs, weatherworn Nissen huts, accommodation blocks, a broken flagpole. Now, in the ditch, he had a sudden attack of the shivers: the place had a creepy feeling. Fen country was different from anywhere else—mile upon mile of flatness, broken only by isolated clumps of trees, and everywhere the dykes. Wartime Britain's unsinkable aircraft-carrier.... Daintree started when the signaller's radio began making noises at him. The signaller twiddled a knob and listened, then reported to the major: 'Aircraft picked up, sir, coming in over Cromer, course 223.'

'Acknowledge.'

Daintree said, 'I'll get back to my lot, Major. But before I go, I'd like to know exactly what your orders are—for when that aircraft touches down?'

'To use my discretion.'

'Attack?'

'No. That's in reserve.'

'A change of orders?'

The major hesitated. 'You chaps are being given a fair crack of the whip. Yes, it's a change in orders.'

'Thank God for that,' Daintree said fervently. 'Keep it that way, Major.' He got to his feet and ran towards his Range Rover, leaving the soldiers to it. His action in moving the spies closer must by now, he fancied, have been reported to Whitehall and had possibly inspired the changed orders. Driving back to his convoy fast before the incoming aircraft arrived over Hatherleigh, Daintree reflected with bitterness on just one of the reasons why, in the first place, he hadn't wanted the armed forces to be used: split command all the way down the line, starting with the Home Office and the Defence Ministry and descending to himself and the major in command of the troops. You could scarcely avoid a lash-up, yet the involvement of the troops had in the end become unavoidable. He reached the police convoy just in time: as he switched off his engine he heard the distant sounds, faintly, the war-reminiscent throb of old-fashioned propeller-engines. In silence they waited. The sounds increased. Soon the aircraft, losing height, was visible, a great dark bird against the cloud, throbbing loudly. For some while it circled, seeking its landing course, familiarizing itself with the whitish gleam of the runways. Keeping well in the cover of the trees Daintree walked past the police vehicles, down the line to take another look at his prisoners. Their faces were showing great strain now. Whatever the official attitude, an attitude which they very well knew, they could not but be feeling that freedom was within a hair's-breadth. In their eyes, as they looked back through the night-dark windows at Daintree, was a wary seeking for information.

The aircraft came in, a perfect three-point landing so far as Daintree could see across the intervening flatness. There was a further roar of sound, then the engines were cut. Looking through field-glasses, Daintree could see no sign of life, no jump down to the ground. Not yet. Possibly not ever. Communication would probably be by radio, with the Home Office, the original contact point for the first telephone call of all, seemingly, now, so long ago.

Daintree, praying to heaven that the infantry major wouldn't be jumping any guns however long he had to wait, climbed back into his Range Rover. The next news came at 01.40, by which time Daintree's nerves were playing him up badly: a message from the Commissioner to Daintree's personal call sign, a message *en clair* since now there was no more need for secrecy: 'Coach driven on to the Forth road bridge from northern approach after shooting down police guard and is now in strong position on centre of bridge.'

For a moment, Daintree put his face in his hands.

* * *

It was, Harkness thought, bloody impregnable apart from all-out military action. The heavy vehicles blocked the approach from north and south in all four lanes—more of them had blasted their way in from both ends of the northbound carriageway as well, so there was a nicely cleared free space to the right of the coach. They were in a fortress, Kahn-built, Kahn-planned. It was clever, and it was terrifying. They were brilliantly lit up, not from the moon alone: from both ends of the bridge, from both approach areas, bright beams shone, playing upon them—searchlights brought up by the Army and mounted high so that they could bear on the lift of the span. In these tattoo-like illuminations, Harkness watched Silver running out his fuse-trails. From the boot of the coach they ran towards the big vehicles—removal vans, they were—stationed at the south perimeter of Kahn's fortress. Here, Harkness lost sight of Silver's activities, but Kahn, not needing to demand the passengers' attention, filled in the blanks.

Standing in his command position in the front of the coach, he stated the facts flatly. 'There's a quantity of high explosive in the boot, primed ready for detonation by fuse. The boot's capacity is around 120 cubic feet, and it's packed tight. The HE is tri-nitro-toluene—TNT—old-fashioned, but effective. There's also a lot of petrol—not, I need hardly say, to propel the coach—just to add to the pyrotechnics.' Kahn grinned, showing his teeth. 'Frying on Monday,' he said, 'or Tuesday, or Wednesday ... I'm a patient man and the deadline's extendable if necessary.' He caught the eye of Harkness. Harkness made an effort, feeling himself the spokesmen of them all.

He asked, 'How long really?'

'You mean, just how patient am I?'

'Yes.'

'Not inexhaustibly, that's for sure. You've all seen Silver laying fuses. If a time comes when I decide your people aren't going to play after all, me and my mates leave the coach, and we leave it locked—from the outside. Soon you'll see Silver welding some attachments to the outside of the doors ... also bars across all windows. We go to the removal vans, and we make one final broadcast on our transmitter, then we light the fuse-trail. That gives you six minutes precisely before it gets too close for *my* safety. If in that time agreement is reached, the fuse can be nipped off. If it isn't ...' Kahn shrugged. 'I don't need to say it, to spell it out, do I? But I'm going to: you'll all fragment. You won't see the bridge go, but a good deal of it will. Five years, wasn't it, of man's ingenuity ... just a heap of metal to block the river. But I believe agreement *will* be reached. And here's another reason why: I'm going to leave a transmitter inside the coach. You can all plead your own case, in person. It'll melt a heart of stone.'

Harkness said, 'You and the others ... Kerrigan, Silver ... you'll all go up with us.' Even as he spoke, he stood in disbelief of his own statement: Kahn would have *that* covered, all right! Kahn, however, wasn't saying how.

* * *

The MacFee daughter, the one whom Harkness had thought looked divorced and was, caught the hot eye of Kerrigan, and smiled. Kerrigan, surprised, smiled back. She moved her head slightly in a come-here gesture.

Kerrigan drifted down the gangway, watchful but interested and stopped beside Agnes MacFee. She was not too attractive, but not too bad either. Keeping her voice down she said, 'I'd like to go outside ... out on the bridge.'

'See the sights, be a tourist? Late—isn't it?'

'I guess I get kind of claustrophobic,' Agnes MacFee said, smiling into his eyes. 'Come with me?'

Kerrigan sucked in breath, pretty sure he had made an accurate interpretation. He felt his blood rise. 'Wait,' he said, recalling his abortive attempt back near Balliemore. He went back up the gangway to the man on watch with him. To his relief, no trouble: it couldn't matter now, and if the woman needed air, okay. Kerrigan looked back and beckoned. Outside on the bridge, with Kerrigan's gun ostentatiously in view, they moved to the back of the coach, blown by a light but cold wind. 'Well?' Kerrigan asked, knowing the answer.

She tossed her hair back, Kerrigan saw the long white gleam of her neck. 'I've seen the way you looked ... what happened back in the barn.'

'Well?' he asked again, smiling. He moistened his lips.

'You want it, don't you?'

He nodded.

She said, 'Well, then, you can have it, I guess.'

'Just like that?'

'Not quite,' she said. Her voice was cold, no emotion at all. 'In exchange for help.'

'What help?'

'Freedom. Life. My parents and me.'

'Freedom?' Kerrigan laughed, a brief sound.

'Not death anyway.' She shivered: in the glare of the searchlights she was already as pale as death. 'Not that. If you won't let us go—and I don't suppose you'll do that—take us with you when you go. Please. Talk to your friends. Maybe they'd all like a woman.'

'You'd do that?'

'For my life, my parents' lives, yes.' She was shivering more now, a violent shake. She put a hand on his arm. 'We wouldn't be a nuisance, I promise. You could drop us off somewhere, I don't know where, just anywhere. It can't hurt you.'

Kerrigan, ready to promise anything, didn't even bother with the words. The woman's mind must have gone, though she'd shown no sign: what would promises be worth? She must be thinking that anything was worth trying, worth a chance at this stage. If it failed to come off, it would be no skin off her nose—not for much longer. Kerrigan grinned, reached, took her suddenly in his arms and pressed his mouth down hard on her lips. She felt stiff, cold, yet, playing her part, not resistant. His hand moved down her body, caressing breasts; his fingers hooked into the hem of her dress, and lifted. The hand touched flesh, warm flesh though her face was still ice cold. She gave a shuddering sigh, but he felt her arms go round him. He had her, out on the bridge, in the beams of the searchlights, with her back against the explosive charges in the boot. He thought: stupid cow. Afterwards he went back with her into the coach, one pace behind, his gun in her back, neither of them speaking. She walked stiff-faced and shaking down the gangway to her seat, looking at no-one, making no protest. Somehow, curiously, Kerrigan felt cheated rather than satisfied.

* * *

From the three trapped cars on their own side, and from one more on the northbound carriageway, new people, new hostages for Kahn, joined the coach later, to stand or sit in the narrow gangway under the careful guns: a representative, a food company's man going home from Dunfermline to Newcastle; a family on an autumn holiday, mother and father and two small children from Yorkshire, also going home; from the Bentley, an important-looking man in tweeds, middle-aged and with a clipped, military manner—a man who was removed by Kahn for questioning in one of the removal vans. In the driving seat cold struck at Harkness, and he shivered, thinking cold thoughts. There was one thing for what it was worth: they were, though isolated still, no longer alone and no longer hidden away from the world's eyes. By morning, they knew, every eye would metaphorically be on the Forth road bridge. Already things were building up, and they could watch them, much as the asphyxiating crew of a sunken submarine might hear the sounds of attempted rescue. Overhead, after a while, aircraft flew low, watching, seeking any useful information. Then a helicopter hovered overhead. Craning their necks, they watched it hopefully, but it flew away again. Down below them on the dark Forth vessels moved busily: two warships, frigates, moved out from HM Dockyard Rosyth and took up positions on either side of the bridge, beaming additional searchlights on Kahn's fortress. Later, when the dawn came, the frigates remained on station, and the people in the coach could see their guns fore and aft, pointing from their turrets towards Kahn's private army. There was enough power there to blast Kahn to kingdom come, but none of it could be used, and they all knew it. But before that dawn had appeared—long before—Kahn had spoken to a waiting world. The Commissioner was at the Home Office, weary from lack of sleep, and hungry, when the voice of Kahn came through:

'This is Tour Eighteen calling... Tour Eighteen calling from the Forth road bridge. My name is Kahn. I am in control, I repeat, I am in control. You will have heard that I crashed the police check-point—you know I am speaking the truth. I have explosives, enough to blow the bridge. I have something else as well, quite by chance—a gentleman by the name of Pendennis. You know him, of course. And you know what I want. It is now in fact fifteen minutes past the deadline—I'm sorry to be unpunctual.' The listeners in Whitehall heard a laugh, a very confident laugh. 'An aircraft is now waiting at Hatherleigh. You will put Cunliffe, Delabier and Massey aboard.' There was a pause. 'Do you hear me? Acknowledge on the following wavelength.' The voice gave the details, then cut out.

The Home Secretary was almost gabbling. 'The bridge—and Pendennis!' Pendennis, Lieutenant-General Sir Hugh Pendennis, commanded the troops in Scotland, had been known to be on his way from Fife to Edinburgh Castle.

The Commissioner lifted an eyebrow. 'May I, sir?' He indicated the transmitting equipment.

'Of course. But be careful. This is for the Prime Minister—'

'I know.' The Commissioner sat in front of the radio transmitter and moved knobs. He spoke into the microphone, with deliberation. 'This is the Commissioner of Metropolitan Police. I am calling Kahn on the Forth road bridge. Do you hear me? Over.'

A click, a buzz. 'I hear you. Do go on.'

'You must wait. I wish to bring in—higher authority.'

'Is this agreement, Commissioner?' Sound rose and fell, listening was not easy.

'It is not agreement. You must give us time—more time.' That, the Commissioner realized the moment he had said it, could be a mistake, an admission that they were half way to being beaten. He went on, 'I hope you realize you can't get away alive yourself unless you release the coach passengers—and General Pendennis. Will you tell me how you got your hands on General Pendennis?'

Kahn explained and added, 'I have two children as well. Ages four and three-and-a-half. Over and out.'

Silence. The Home Secretary looked ill, sick, out of his depth. He said as if to himself. 'If the bridge goes...'

'We must talk to the Prime Minister,' the Commissioner said. On this point there was agreement. The Home Secretary called Downing Street personally. Putting down the telephone he said, 'He's coming himself.'

The Commissioner's hand began tapping on the arm of the radio operator's chair.

* * *

In the coach they listened to the discussion of their own fate: Kahn had brought the transceiver equipment across from one of the removal vans and Silver, a man of parts, had rigged an aerial. It came over audibly enough from London, only slightly affected by atmospherics.

'This is the Prime Minister. You are making most impudent demands which will not be met.' A strong pause. 'Over.'

'I think,' Kahn said, 'they will. About a ton of TNT plus petrol says they will. In the morning, Prime Minister, I shall make contact with the press—'

'So you're extending the time limit?' There was pounce in the Prime Minister's voice as he used his switch and cut in, pounce and a degree of triumphant I-told-you-so.

'The time-limit was always flexible, but there's a break point which you would be unwise to discount. I'm easy up to a point, but I won't be trifled with. I realize you need time. That's all. Meanwhile I shall tell you more fully what I want.' Kahn paused, squinting a little in the glare of the searchlights. 'When the aircraft takes off—with Cunliffe, Delabier and Massey aboard—its flight will not be interfered with. When it reaches its destination, *safely*, I shall be informed. When I am so informed, and not before, I shall release all hostages. Or rather, let me put it this way.' Kahn grinned down the gangway. "They'll be left in the coach, alone, no guards. They will not be *safe* until my own personal party, like the aircraft, is beyond your power to arrest. You ask how this is? I shall tell you: the TNT and the petrol can be blown two ways. One, by fuse. Two, by remote control—by radio. You understand, Prime Minister? The moment I look like being interfered with, up goes the coach and the bridge. And that, for now, is all I have to say. Out!'

* * *

The Prime Minister pushed his chair back, away from the broadcast equipment. He mopped at his face and made an astonishing statement. 'I think they're weakening,' he said.

'I wouldn't bank on *that*, sir!'

'No, no. Not bank. But I think they are, all the same. They've let the deadline pass, haven't they?'

The Commissioner shrugged. 'I doubt if that means much, sir. The first deadline could have been designed simply to get us moving . . . past experience tells me that hijackers usually do have flexible deadlines in any case. There's no reason for them to weaken and I don't accept that they are—on the contrary, they're in a very strong position, and there's nothing we can do about it. I hate to admit this . . . but the plain fact is, they've got the better of us so far.'

'Defeatist talk,' the Prime Minister said pettishly. 'We'll have none of that, Commissioner.' Once again he mopped his face, seemed, despite brave words, to be sunk in misery. He said, 'The bridge, Home Secretary.'

'Yes, sir.'

'One of the main routes north—all that chaos! So much traffic from the ports. All those years of hard work.'

'There are people on the bridge, sir,' the Commissioner reminded him. 'Lives.'

The Prime Minister looked up, his eyes clouded. 'Yes, yes, I know. I have every sympathy . . . but it's virtually a symbol, a symbol to the world of what we British can do—the road bridge. The greatest feat of our time! It would be such an appalling tragedy!' He shook his head, then seemed to take a grip, to strengthen his resolution: it was an almost visible process. The head went back, the lower lip jutted, the colour heightened. 'You spoke of them getting the better of us, Commissioner. What we have to concentrate on now is getting the better of *them*, and they're giving us time, aren't they?'

There was a silence. The last utterance was the Prime Ministerly equivalent of military buck-passing . . . the Commissioner asked patiently but pointedly, 'Have *you* any ideas, sir?'

'Yes,' the Prime Minister answered. 'Play for time, keep them guessing, concentrate troops at both ends of the bridge, in the approaches . . . have all RAF operational units warned for immediate take-off, and have plenty of warships in the river. And,' he added, 'watch Cunliffe, Delabier and Massey like a hawk! What's the name of your man?'

'Daintree, sir.'

'Yes, Daintree. He really knows his job?'

The Commissioner nodded. 'The very best, sir. Wholly dependable.'

'Good.' The Prime Minister, who had seemed about to say something further, hesitated and didn't say it. He went to the door and said good-night. Back to bed, the Commissioner thought, tired as all hell himself—back to bed to worry about the bridge. And what he'd left unsaid . . . the Commissioner had an idea the Prime Minister didn't want to commit himself to anything in particular but that he wouldn't be asking too many questions about the relevant doings of Commander Daintree, who might by unorthodox methods be able to get him out of a nasty spot. It was interesting to speculate: *why hadn't the Prime Minister ordered the spies back to prison?* Popularity Jack was still on the vote-catch . . . Another thought struck the Commissioner: would the Prime Minister find it acceptable if Cunliffe, Delabier and Massey were actually to escape and make their way aboard the waiting aircraft? Afterwards, the police could always take the blame! But that was far too dangerous an accusation, much too dangerous to be voiced—and perhaps from the Prime Minister's viewpoint too blatant a face-saver. All the same. . . .

The Commissioner pulled himself up sharply: a policeman must never think along those lines—never. Meanwhile, the Prime Minister was due for another bad press tomorrow or the next day—Kahn's spiel would be in time for the evening paper this fateful day of Monday, probably. Perhaps that—plus the bridge—would loosen the official view . . . the Commissioner was finding himself convinced that the spies must be handed over. So many lives were at stake, including that of an important senior Army officer, a VIP, now. A vital road link between England and the north was also threatened. A public execution in the middle of the Firth of Forth, a spectacle —and God knew it would be that, with the central portion of the bridge rising to the heavens in a sheet of flame and a belch of smoke, to fall back, shattered, into the water—a spectacle for the watching, like some Roman lion-fed sacrifice, by massed thousands along the banks of the Forth and on the world's television screens, was not to be borne.

The Commissioner, about to share his thoughts with the

Home Secretary, stopped with his mouth open as a telephone shrilled. The Home Secretary answered and handed the instrument to the Commissioner. 'For you.'

The Commissioner listened. 'Commissioner here,' he said. 'Daintree...'

'Daintree!' The Commissioner caught his breath. 'You sound all in. What's the matter?'

'Sir... I'm calling from the police station at Fencantwell, near Hatherleigh. Cunliffe and the others—they've gone.'

The Commissioner, white faced, stared across the room unseeingly. 'Gone? Escaped? To the aircraft?'

'I don't think so. The aircraft hasn't taken off, to my knowledge. The police convoy was attacked... I believe this is where Moscow comes in.'

13

'WE DIDN'T have a chance,' Daintree said. His fingers strayed to his throat: it was still sore, and the bruises were coming out. He was talking to the Commissioner, in the Fencantwell police station—the local constable's house. 'They came like shadows... like they used to in India, in the days of *thuggee*.'

'I gather you were outnumbered?'

'Three to one,' Daintree said bitterly. All this was sheer gall. To lose one prisoner was to lose all face: to lose three prisoners of the political weight of Cunliffe, Delabier and Massey was total failure. 'Carried out with military precision, no bungling. Each of us was an individual target, I fancy—for three men. No shooting—there wasn't time. They had knives, but didn't need to use them. A bloodless victory if ever there was one!'

'Any known faces?'

Daintree laughed, more bitter than ever. 'They were all masked—all hooded. A black hood over each man's head, with eye slits. And they didn't utter—not a bloody word! No, no known faces, sir.'

'You mentioned a Moscow involvement, on the phone—'

'Yes, I did. But that's supposition—because of what one of my contacts... the woman... told me. I can't be precise, but...'

'Well?'

Daintree said, 'On reflection, sir, I'm inclined to discount Moscow.'

'Why?'

'From their point of view, wouldn't it have been better to have attacked the hijackers after they'd got our three villains? I mean—'

'You mean less of a political involvement. Well, I'm with

you there! On the other hand, Moscow wouldn't have been able to predict what we would do with the spies, Daintree. They may have taken the main chance—simply that. To Some extent Cunliffe, Delabier and Massey were sitting on a plate, weren't they?'

Daintree groaned. 'Well enough put, sir. And it's my fault.'

The Commissioner said, 'Don't forget I backed you. That stands. We won't do any crying over spilt milk—time's far too short! We have to get them back, Daintree.' The Commissioner moved over to the window, looked out on a peaceful village green, wet with the dawn's dew. Light stole over trees beyond the green, a belt of elms. To the east the sky was shot with emerging colour, pink, mauve, green. Somewhere over there, Kahn's aircraft waited still: still under hidden surveillance from the troops, whose officer had sent reports by runner—no noisy despatch-riders—at intervals throughout the night. No-one had been seen to emerge from that aircraft, the reports said. There was light in it, and that was all. Neither had any radio transmissions from it been picked up on the monitors. Turning, the Commissioner repeated, 'We have to get them back, Daintree. You're still in charge. In the meantime . . . what the devil do we tell the Prime Minister?'

Daintree lifted his palms, took a long breath, sent it whistling out again through his teeth. 'What do we tell Kahn?' he asked.

* * *

Silver had carried out more night work. In one of the removal vans had been welding equipment and a generator. Silver busily and skilfully welded bars across all the windows of the coach, his efforts aided by the brilliance of the searchlights. When the windows were effectively sealed, he attended to the doors, welding heavy bolts into position. As he worked, his blinding flame played across the faces of the passengers. Down the centre of the coach, the newcomers were questioned by Kerrigan and Rubery. Kahn was absent, in one of the vans, engaged once again with the VIP, General Pendennis. Kerrigan and Rubery were interrupted continually by crying from the two small children who, uncomprehending of disaster, wanted only to go to bed, proper bed, with no intruding light. Some of the original passengers—Ernie Peach, the MacFees—had given up their own seats for use by the children as makeshift beds, but this didn't seem to fill the bill. Rubery shushed at them and went on with the questions.

'What's the feeling outside?'

'The feeling?' This was the food rep. 'How d'you mean, the feeling?'

Rubery swept an arm around the coach. 'Them—and you, now. Your deaths, friend! What do people think?'

'About you?'

Rubery laughed. 'Not about me. We can guess that part! About—shall we say—the obstinacy of officialdom.'

The rep, a sandy, thin man named John Perkinshaw, said, 'They're shocked. It hasn't happened before in Britain—not like this. There was that business a few years ago at Heathrow, but it didn't have the impact—'

'So this has?'

Perkinshaw nodded. 'Yes, I'd say so.'

'When you say shocked,' Rubery asked, 'do you mean shocked about the hijack itself, or shocked about Cunliffe, Delabier and Massey not being handed over—that being, to date, the official publicized line?'

'Both.'

'What do you think they'll do?'

'I don't know...'

Rubery said, 'You're a rep, a commercial traveller. You get around, you talk to people. You must have formed some impressions.'

'Well, perhaps. But I don't know... I don't talk to people whose opinion matters very much, you know. I think the feeling seems to be that those three men aren't worth a lot of people...' Perkinshaw didn't seem able to get out the word, dying: it was too personal now. He looked around in awe; it was rather like seeing at close hand, for the first time, people like the lunarnauts, or royalty, or a TV personality. Beside him was an old man with a white moustache, a man who looked like real class—probably he was old Lord Hanborough, the one who had made the first telephone contact. There was the blind man with the stick... they were all personalities, hogging the press these last few days. Now he was one of them. Perkinshaw's knees weakened, and he sagged against a seat-back. His mouth wobbling he said, 'I hope to God the bloody politicians see sense, I hope to God they do! Why should any of us die for three bloody traitors?'

* * *

It was still the responsibility of Harkness to attend to the periodic emptying of the chemical lavatory. Here on the bridge the contents had to be lifted across the guardrail and committed to the waters of the Firth of Forth. After a breakfast of stale bread, one apple each, and a little water, Harkness moved to the rear of the coach, brought out the can, carried it with difficulty through the press of people in the gangway, smelling chemically. At the front, one of Rubery's uniformed men watched the manoeuvre. As Harkness moved past Hanborough, the old man put out a hand as paper-white as his face, halting Harkness.

'Can I help?' he asked.

Harkness smiled. 'Good heavens, no, I can manage, thanks all the same.' He looked down. Hanborough, he fancied, had a brighter look, and that was good. He seemed to have taken a grip again. Harkness, starting to move on, said, 'I like the exercise anyway.'

'Fresh air,' Hanborough said. 'I need that.' He pulled himself to his feet, mouth working, eyes bright.

Harkness stopped again, full of compassion. He said, 'Far as I'm concerned, you can come if you want, sir. It's not up to us, though, is it?'

'I wonder if you'd ask that fellow in the front?'

'Sure I will.' Harkness pushed past the pair from the dormobile, bearing his unpleasant burden towards the door. He spoke to the guard, asking and getting permission for old Hanborough to breathe fresh air. He called back to Hanborough, who moved stiffly through for the door, joining Harkness. They got down on to the carriageway and approached the guardrail together.

They looked down past a massive steel beam, down a long way to the water. Harkness lifted his bucket, tipped it, watched the contents snake down, splashing off the steel into the Firth of Forth, and saw one of the on-station frigates with men on her bridge scanning the carriageway through binoculars. Above, two helicopters moved in from easterly: aboard them men were busy, aiming equipment at the coach and its surroundings. Unknowing, as he looked upward, Harkness stared into the lenses of cameras of a BBC Television film unit and of an Outside Broadcasts crew. Beside him, Hanborough sniffed keen air, filling creaky lungs, wheezing a little.

'A beautiful day...'

'Yes.'

'I don't think we're going to get out of this, Harkness.'

'Never say die, sir.' Wrong choice of word!

'Ah—but that's it, isn't it? I think we all have to face it now. What's more—it's *right*.'

'Right?' Harkness stared.

'The country can't give in to blackmail. Surely that's obvious? It would lead to so many similar situations. We must regard ourselves as soldiers, Harkness, soldiers of the Queen, engaged upon a warlike operation. I—'

'That's all very well for you. You've been a soldier. Others haven't, me included.'

'Then now's your chance, Harkness.' The old man coughed, a hollow sound. Harkness looked at him curiously: the eyes looked funny, he thought, kind of over-excited... Hanborough went on cryptically, 'As I see it, there's only one way we can affect the situation positively. It'll be an individual decision, of course, but I would hope that by example I can influence the other passengers. Tell me, Harkness, can you get a message to General Pendennis?'

'Well, I don't know.' Harkness, feeling a sense of danger, danger in any crack-brained plan from past and forgotten wars, scratched his head and decided to procrastinate for the time being. 'That Kahn... he's got General Pendennis in one of those vans still. Maybe when he comes back... but can't you talk to him yourself?'

'With so many listening ears, Harkness? Come now! Kahn's

bound to see us talking, or one of his men is. I think it's up to you—perhaps when doing latrine duty, you know. Find an excuse to take Pendennis with you.' He coughed again. Harkness was aware of an increased beat from his heart, an increased flow of blood that came from his feeling of being pressured. In spite of his natural fears the other way, he had a kind of faith, a belief deep in his bones that in the end the authorities would cave in. In the meantime, his duty to Mary and the children was to stay alive and not indulge in heroics—not unless they stood a real chance. Something told him unmistakably that schemes of poor old Hanborough's would not stand that essential chance. But it would be unkind to say the least, to let the old man know this.

Harkness said uneasily, 'Depends what the message is, I reckon. Want to tell me . . . want to trust me with it, in case I get a chance to pass it on?'

Hanborough nodded, and put a hand lightly on Harkness's shoulder, just for a moment. 'Good man! Yes, of course I'll trust you.' He coughed again. 'Tell the General we need to disperse, Harkness—'

'Disperse?'

'Yes. That's it. Disperse. Do away with the enemy's bargaining counters. I know Pendennis will see it that way too—damn it, he's a Sandhurst man, not one of these university intellectuals—he's a soldier, as I am. You'll tell him, Harkness?'

'Yes . . . I'll tell him. But I don't know that I understand. In fact I bloody *know* I don't.'

Hanborough said quietly, 'It will all come clear. May happiness attend you and yours, Harkness, my dear fellow.' He held out a hand, which Harkness took. The old man's grip was surprisingly strong and firm—almost young. 'It's a very beautiful day, Harkness, isn't it?'

'It is that,' Harkness agreed.

'All those people,' Hanborough said, waving a hand towards the northern bank of the Firth. 'Quite extraordinary, don't you think?' Harkness turned to look: not until now aware of them, he gasped when he saw the crowds. On every vantage point, down by South Queensferry, by Abercorn, wherever you cared to look, life and the colour of gay clothing, red, green, blue, white—gaiety in the forefront of death's arena, in the grandstand view. Already the ghouls had gathered. Harkness felt sick. He stared in a kind of fascination. While he was staring, Hanborough took his chance—took Harkness totally by surprise, though afterwards he told himself again and again that he should have realized, should have got the drift of craziness. Hanborough, the white, bristly stubble shining in the early sunlight on his faded cheeks—after arrival on the bridge, shaving had ceased—had somehow heaved himself up bodily on to the guardrail; and before Harkness could move, he had dropped over. Harkness, gripping the wide barrier in stark horror, watched as though he couldn't look away, and saw the whole terrible ending. Hanborough's body, after bouncing off the bridge structure between carriageway and footway, went down with the arms and legs spread and the white hair standing up in the down-draught whenever his body came upright. Over and over, spiralling towards the rippled water. Not a dive: the water—and this he would know—would break his back like a reed. But in the event it was not the water he hit: the guarding frigate had moved a little, had come inwards towards the bridge. Hanborough hit the fo'c'sle-head and lay there, lay still and shattered in a spreading pool of blood, across the white-painted links of the anchor cable, his head split like a fallen coconut on the rough steel of a bottle-screw slip. His feet as heavy as lead Harkness turned away, feeling, sickly, that he too must fall unless he got back in the coach. Before he turned away he heard a curious distant sound, not quite a roar, more like a huge-scale sigh, that came from those massed, rubbernecking crowds along the Firth.

Stumbling, sick, horrified, Harkness made the coach, having the dream-feel of weighted legs and receding targets, of the place you never got to. No-one aboard the coach had seen, not even the man with the gun up front. As it happened, all attention had been on the upstream movements of a naval vessel coming out of Rosyth... but now Harkness's white face told a story: questions came. Where was Hanborough?

'He fell in,' Harkness, said, shaking. 'He fell in, poor old bugger.' He looked up, saw the disbelief: old men didn't exactly fall over high guardrails. Harkness said, 'All right. He jumped. It's all over now anyway, so what's the odds?' He went back to the toilet compartment with the emptied bucket, clanging it back in place, a knell for poor old Hanborough he thought with bitter sadness. He understood now, but he would say nothing. Nor would he pass any messages to General Pendennis, except, if he ever did get the chance, to put things square for Hanborough. Crazy! Kahn, after all, wasn't grass-green enough to fall for it. Yet a courageous concept, however crazy and impossible, and with its own curious basis of logic: if Kahn had no hostages left, the government wouldn't need to cave in.

* * *

The night before, arrangements had been made to start the next day's television broadcasts earlier than normal, while existing programmes would be interrupted with news flashes as necessary. Thus in the world beyond the Forth Hanborough's death was a live television sensation: the BBC had got it all beautifully, clear as day when the helicopters had tracked back east of the bridge. In Downing Street the Prime Minister had a personal grandstand view. He watched with a glum face, in horror, as Hanborough hit the frigate's steel deck; he watched in fear for the effect this was going to have upon the public. When the cameras, shifting their focus from the frigate to the carriageway of the bridge, brought up the coach, the Prime Minister saw a short, square man getting back in with a bucket; and saw the faces of the passengers behind the glass of the windows. Frightened faces, hopeless faces, faces, with death written upon them. The cameras tracked along the great bridge to the crowded northern approach, showing the troops and police and vehicles, the fire-fighting equipment, the ambulances. The Prime Minister scarcely heard the commentary, uttered in hushed funereal tones, the whole weighty majesty of Dimbleby-Michelmore mobilized for the occasion: the stark picture was more than enough to exacerbate anxiety. Later in the day it was fully reported on the BBC News and ITN broadcasts, but, by personal direction of the Prime Minister, the recorded film of Hanborough's dreadful end was cut to lie unused in its can. Of that, enough had been seen already. That live broadcast hadn't exactly caused uproar in the streets: this, after all, was Britain. But public opinion had hardened as a result of it. That opinion hardened both ways at once: vermin must not be allowed to get away with blackmail; on the other side of the opinion fence, the surviving coach passengers must be put out of their misery at once—and the ending of that, via surrender, lay firmly in the hands of the government.

This left the Prime Minister in more of a dilemma than ever, especially since the disappearance of Cunliffe, Delabier and Massey—a fact on which there was now a total security clampdown.

14

KAHN didn't react too strongly to Hanborough's suicide jump; in his view, it could help his position, if anything. But he did put a ban on further excursions from the coach. In the case of persons more active than old Hanborough, such could lead to more than suicide. Kahn was still entirely confident of success: indeed, it seemed to Harkness that the hijack boss was even more confident than before and was more relaxed, more chatty. He had come back to the coach with Pendennis and though there was no indication that he had learned anything from the latter in any positive sense, he remarked to the armed guard in the front that the authorities were satisfactorily rocked by events. As Pendennis found a place in the gangway to squat, Kahn had a word with Harkness, referring back to Hanborough.

'Stupid, that. He'd have been free, soon.'

'I don't think he wanted to be. Not without his wife.'

Kahn laughed. 'Does anybody *want* to die?'

No answer to that. Harkness said, 'I think he'd have pegged out before long, anyway. Or gone right round the bend.' He looked up at Kahn, at the hard, dark face, the sadistic eyes. 'How long is this going to go on?'

'It's not up to me... is it?'

'You can't hold out indefinitely and you know it.'

'Do I?' Kahn smiled, shook his head. 'Indefinitely doesn't come into it, friend. Soon, I'll force them—give a hard deadline that'll be kept to. But in the meantime, it pays to let them simmer. Time's on my side, not theirs. The longer it goes on, the more public opinion will react, and there's nothing your government can do against us. Isn't that obvious by now?'

Once again there seemed to be no answer to the truth.

Harkness sat glumly behind the wheel while Kahn got down again and went on a tour of his removal vans. By now the reels of barbed wire had been used to make a barricade at either end of Kahn's strongpoint. Any attack along the bridge would be halted there, and Kahn's guns would find good targets. Harkness, looking ahead past the removal vans, saw activity on the carriageways—police and troops coming up with revolvers and rifles and what looked like light artillery; but they halted well clear, establishing a line some two hundred yards from the barricade. Harkness twisted round to look behind: a similar manoeuvre was taking place from the northern bridge approach.

Harkness drew no comfort from the proximity of power: it was powerless power. Those guns could not be used, and everyone must know it. It was just a charade: if there was no surrender they were going to die and that was all about it. Harkness, shivering with cold now, unwashed and unshaven and feeling desperately unclean to add to a creeping demoralization, found his mind wandering back to Hanborough. At least the old man had made a clean, quick end of it.

* * *

'Word from the Prime Minister,' the Commissioner said on the telephone to Daintree. 'Re Cunliffe, Delabier and Massey. No stone to be left unturned. Your name's mud, so is mine. If anything leaks to the hijackers, he'll have our livers out. And I doubt if they're going to be in ignorance for long, somehow!'

'You're right,' Daintree said. 'I suppose he's seething—'

'He's fermenting. Damn it, I don't blame him. Get them, Daintree, pull out all the stops!'

'Of course.' Daintree wanted to snap, but kept his voice even. 'What's been done—the broad spectrum?'

'The usual form. Keep in touch.' The Commissioner rang off. Daintree tapped his fingers on his desk. The usual: ports and airports, road blocks that had been set up within fifteen minutes of his initial report from Fencantwell, but to no avail ... and the rest up to Daintree, all of it, apart from the above-ground diplomatic approaches, and *they* wouldn't be worth the time taken. Daintree felt defeated, knew he faced a long slog and believed there wouldn't be the time, not short of a monumental stroke of luck. Cunliffe, Delabier and Massey could be anywhere in all Britain, or even out of it if their abductors, like the hijack outfit, had an aircraft ready somewhere. But this Daintree felt he could discount: there had been no reports from the radar defences of any unscheduled flights out. And they wouldn't have had a hope in hell of getting out by way of any scheduled flights. The net would have been very tight-drawn, full inspection of outward cargo crates being just one of the routines of a first-class national emergency.

Inside Britain, then. Russian Embassy? If so, the situation was dicey in the extreme. But Daintree didn't feel the Russians would take that kind of risk, not even for three top-grade spies and their know-how. In their way, embassies were as vital as spies as a source of necessary information, and they were more permanent, just so long as ambassadors were allowed to remain in their host countries. The satellite embassies? Same principle applied, if to a lesser degree in the eyes of Moscow.

A possibility?

Daintree drummed the desk, plagued by uncertainties. He was half hoping that the woman, Esther Marko, would make contact. He waited a while in case she did. Experience told him that it would be useless and dangerous for him to initiate the contact: if she knew anything, if she wished to impart it, she would be in touch. When his telephones remained silent Marko-wise, Daintree got up and went out to begin his own part in that long, long slog, the slog that had been started by his patient officers the moment his first report had reached the Yard.

* * *

Questions, questions everywhere. In Soho, for instance, things were often to be picked up, little things that might lead to bigger ones. Cafes, public houses, knocking shops, porn shops, strip joints, anywhere the fringe people gathered. Listen and look, ask, hand out the cash, and hope, hope, hope.

Follow up leads, however slim, hope again and find disappointment. This time, Daintree's departmental officers had a special interest, the fate of the coach passengers quite apart: their branch was impugned and their chief was in dead trouble if he didn't produce like a conjuror. And Daintree they regarded highly, so it was a case of a very hard try. It all led, by the end of that first evening of search, to damn-all: no-one, if they knew anything and this was doubtful since it was out of the normal run of their experience, was opening his or her mouth. Understandable: Moscow's arm was a long one. The straight police forces got nowhere either: on the lookout, on the rake-through in all corners of Britain, they turned up total blanks.

Daintree, near despair though he'd known the job would be a long one, snatched three hours' sleep in his office, then started again. He went, in the middle of the night, to Pentonville, home of the spies before they had been shifted. The Governor, brought out of his bed by a warning telephone call, spoke to Daintree in his office.

'What is it you want?' he asked.

'The associates of Cunliffe, Delabier and Massey. The ones they were particularly friendly with. Also the ones they were particularly *un*friendly with.' Daintree, like a caged animal, paced the office backwards and forwards, reduced now to nail-biting. His face looked ghastly in the electric light.

'You know cons as well as I do, Commander.'

'You mean they don't talk. I have to make them—that's all!'

'If they know anything to talk about.'

Daintree moved his shoulders irritably. 'I'm aware of all that. Will you please just have them sorted out and lined up for me? That's all I ask of you, Mr Stone.'

'You'll—er—act properly, with circumspection?'

Daintree laughed, a bitter laugh. 'Do I look that far gone? You can check me for lead piping if you like, blunt instruments, the lot.' He added, 'Before I see the men concerned, I'll want their files. I'll need to know all about them.'

'I'm—'

'All the responsibility will be mine.'

The Governor nodded, gave the necessary orders. Daintree waited, a prey to his nerves. He knew he could do more or less as he liked that night, always provided he was in the end successful. He would have the highest backing and not too many questions would be asked. Nevertheless, he told himself, there would be no physical methods: that, in any situation, was beyond the bounds. But he would shrink from no mental pressures to bring *something* out into the light of day, something, however small, that might start a progressive trail. Waiting for the files to come, he knew it was a long shot: cons were cons, put away for all kinds of reasons, not many of them political. Besides, it was doubtful if even Cunliffe, Delabier and Massey themselves would have been aware that there was a plot to hook them off to Moscow. If that was what it was, and even that wasn't one hundred per cent certain: such a plot must have been hastily put together after the news of the hijack reached the hookers-off. All the same, it was a stone that could bear turning over: nothing could be left out now.

The files came—ten of them, dividing on the word of the prison's Chief Officer into four known friends and six known enemies of Cunliffe and Delabier. Of Massey, none. Massey was a man who walked alone, uncommunicative, making neither friends nor enemies. Carefully, Daintree studied all the files, noting, reflecting, working up a line. Inside an hour, he had all the details in his mind. He looked up at the Governor and Chief Officer, both yawning their heads off.

'Ready,' he said. 'Singly, of course, in a cell with a table, a chair and an anglepoise lamp.' He saw the look that passed between the two officers, knew they hated this. But he was going to do it his way, the way he had done it with Cunliffe, Delabier and Massey themselves. He added, handing over a file, 'This one first.' The file was that of a con named Edgar William Blunt, category enemy of Cunliffe, a man whom Daintree happened to know, a man put away on conviction for drug smuggling as an end result of certain of Daintree's own successful investigations three years previously. A man who could be considered to have touched the periphery of international affairs...

Daintree was taken to his interrogation cell, where he

arranged the lamp as he wanted it. Blunt was brought in, under heavy guard. The cell was very silent: Daintree could hear his own wrist-watch tick. He asked the questions in a quiet voice, slowly at first, then faster, making use of the file information, patiently threatening. After fifteen minutes he knew it was useless: Blunt knew nothing. Daintree was convinced of that. He could not afford wasted time. He dismissed Blunt, sent for the next, then the next... Pulling out all those stops, Daintree pressed hard, threatening ominous things—prison beatings when the hostages died, harsher treatment from prison officers, no let-up, loss of privileges, loss of remission—going beyond the bounds, maybe weakening his own case by over-threats that would not be carried out, even using the men's families, even promising deeper investigations into un-cleared-up matters from the past, and longer sentences. He felt himself shaking, felt—knew—he was letting the strain show, letting it affect his judgment.

He got nowhere with the friends and enemies of Cunliffe and Delabier and in the end, when he was on the brink of giving up, the break-through came via Massey, almost fortuitously. He was interrogating a small man, skinny and rat-like, a man said to hate Delabier, when a pinpoint emerged.

'That Massey..."

'A friend of yours?'

'Not a friend.' The small man shook his head, bead-like eyes squinting in the bright light. 'I used to see... a bloke visited him... oh, twice, maybe three times, I dunno really.'

'Well?'

'Well, Massey used to like, *talk* to himself. Sort of nervous he was, you know? Specially after this bloke had been to visit. Something about bloody Czechs.'

'What, exactly, did he say?'

'Dunno really. Just muttered. Bloody Czechs was about all I got.' An introspective look came into the face. 'Just a minute, though. Didn't want no trouble, he said once. Didn't want no trouble, didn't want no questions. Just do his porridge—serve his time. That's it. I remember now.'

'Anything else?'

'No. Honest. That was all I got. He just muttered, like, into his beard.'

'This man, this visitor, was he a foreigner?'

'No, I don't think so. Looked sort of British.'

'Description?'

The eyes screwed up, into the light, seeking Daintree. 'Tallish, just under six foot. Big built... big stomach. Grey hair... nearly white. Sort of pink complexion. Well fed. A nob, like.'

More questions, but the ratty man had said his lot, he knew nothing further. Daintree dismissed him and saw the remainder of the cons with half his mind on tallish, stomachy, white-haired, pink-faced, well-fed nobs. Not an unusual combination, nothing spectacular... Daintree, ending the long interrogation session, went back to the Governor's office, riding on a sixth sense. Massey, he found when lists were brought, had had few visitors. On three occasions he had been visited by a man named Salisbury—Mr, not Marquis of. On a numerical basis, that seemed to fit; but the name hadn't got to be the genuine one. In fact it probably wasn't, if Daintree's sixth sense, strongly aroused by the reference to Czechs, was correct.

Back to Esther Marko?

* * *

First the Commissioner, anxious for news as soon as Daintree reached his office. Daintree was buzzed for, and went to make his report.

'Blank but for that?'

'As blank as a baby's bottom, sir, but I think this one's good.'

'Tallish, big stomach, white hair, pink face, a well-fed nob,' the Commissioner reflected slowly. 'Could be the Prime Minister!'

A wintry smile: 'I'd doubt that.'

'My apologies. What's your next step?'

'I have a contact in the... required direction, sir. The woman. Somewhat uncertain. I'd have expected some word before now, the circumstances being what they are.' Daintree rubbed at weary, red-rimmed eyes. 'I'll be trying, never fear.'

Back to his office and the telephone. He called the M.P. at whose house he had met Esther Marko. The M.P. was in his bath. Was it, the wife asked, important? Daintree said, very.

'Is it about . . . you know who?'

Bloody adverts! It was catching, and it was too stupidly amateurishly undercover . . . Daintree cursed his nerves: the poor woman *was* an amateur and didn't know what it was all about anyway. He said, 'Yes, that's right.'

The voice, distrait, weepy all of a sudden, said shatteringly, 'She's dead. My husband was going to ring the police.'

Daintree felt his stomach drain away.

15

THE M.P. wasn't in his bath: that had been just a wifely protective answer. Daintree, however, didn't speak to him on the phone: he went round, pronto. The wife let him in.

'Where's the body?' he demanded brusquely and without preliminaries.

'In the study.'

Daintree went to the study. The M.P. was there, ashen-faced, downing a stiff whisky. Early for whisky, but he looked as though he needed it badly. By the window, which had one pane of glass spider's-webbed around a neat hole, lay the body. Daintree went over and knelt by it, feeling, as a routine measure, for heartbeats: there were none. Blood had flowed from the back of the head and gathered in a pool, sticky on the thick carpet. Daintree looked up. 'How did it happen?'

The M.P. waved his whisky tumbler at the window. 'It's obvious, isn't it?'

'Perhaps. Your own words, please. This is vitally important. I haven't words to say just how important.'

The tumbler was drained, knuckles rubbed into eyes, the tumbler was refilled: a lifted eyebrow asked wordlessly if Daintree would care for a drink?

'Thank you, no. Get on with it—the story.'

'Yes, of course.' The M.P. took a gulp of the whisky, remained standing, looking down at the body. 'Esther Marko ... she came to see me. It was unexpected—she rang first, but it was basically unexpected—you know?'

'What did she want?'

'I don't know, Commander. She said on the phone, it was vitally important—your own phrase just now. That's all I know'. He indicated the bullet hole in the window. 'That happened first, you see.'

'She'd only just got here, then?'

'Yes. I—'

'Who let her in, you or your wife?'

'I did.' The M.P. anticipated the next question. 'I didn't see anyone else. No-one else at all—the street was empty.'

'You took her straight to the study—straight here?'

'Yes. She was ... agitated. Very agitated. She wouldn't sit down—'

'Stood, back to the window? Foolish!'

'Not *close*. I had just asked her to sit down, as a matter of fact, and she just happened to ... well, be standing like that when she answered.'

'What did she answer?'

'Oh, just said there wasn't time to stop.' The M.P.'s voice shook. 'The next second she was dead. Or very nearly. She staggered a little, moved back towards the window ... and then she fell. I haven't moved her, by the way.'

Daintree nodded, still kneeling by the body. 'You heard the shot?'

'Not a thing. I imagine there was a silencer.'

'Very likely. When did this happen?'

'Only minutes before you rang.' The M.P. looked at his watch. 'Half an hour ago.'

'So it'd have been light, daylight.'

'Yes.'

Daintree indicated the window; the curtains were open. 'Were the curtains drawn at that time?'

'No. I drew them back when I came in with Esther Marko.'

'Did you see *anything*, before or after it happened?'

'Not a thing.'

'Did you go out to look, afterwards?'

The M.P. didn't meet Daintree's eye. 'Not out. I did look from the window but I didn't see anyone. There's a gate at the end of the garden ... it gives on to a service alley. It wouldn't take anyone long to get away.'

'I suppose not,' Daintree said sourly. He got to his feet and examined the hole in the glass: a heavy calibre bullet, by the look of it. Forensic would be able to deduce the make of gun, for what help that would be; the bullet itself would still be in the head. Daintree swung round. 'Any theories?' he asked.

'I don't think so.'

'Try. Try hard, please. You knew the woman, I didn't—just that one meeting the other day—remember? Do you see a connection?'

The M.P. shrugged. 'Really, I just don't know. I told you, she hadn't time to say a thing.'

'But from your own knowledge? Tell me, what was the set-up? How did you come to know her in the first place?'

'Through my work.'

'Which is—apart from the House? Or do you mean via the House?'

'No. I'm a committee member of the International Political Freedom League.'

Daintree, who happened to know this, nodded absently. 'She's a member too?'

'No. That didn't suit her embassy. But she's—she was sympathetic.'

'Yes, I see. Did she ever tell you anything . . . give you any information that might be pertinent?'

'Pertinent to what? She never revealed any what you might call secrets—no. I wasn't on a spying mission anyway.'

'But she trusted you—enough to use your house as a place to meet me. You just asked, pertinent to what?' Daintree faced the man squarely. 'I'm going to tell you, but you must allow me, first, to quote the Official Secrets Act. What I'm going to tell you is between you and me alone—no-one else at all. You do understand?'

'Yes.'

'Did she tell you what she wanted to see me about?'

'No. And I didn't ask, Commander.'

Daintree nodded. 'Good. Here it is. There's a connection between Esther Marko—between her death too—and the coach at present held on the Forth road bridge. If there is anything you can tell me, bearing that in mind . . . it could save very many lives. Well?'

The M.P.'s eyes widened. 'Good God!' he said. He stared

down at the body, incredulously. There was no acting: the man was clearly, genuinely surprised and shocked. 'I never knew ... she didn't ever refer to anything like that.'

'Or anything that could now connect? In retrospect?'

'No ... no, I'm sure not. I can't think of anything.'

Daintree nodded, concealing disappointment. 'I see. If anything does occur, let me know immediately.' He added, 'Does the name Salisbury mean anything to you?'

'Salisbury?'

'Not the peer, not the town. Just a man called Salisbury.' He paused. 'No?'

'No.'

Daintree hesitated. Once again, the name could be false. But it was difficult to obtain recognition from a bald description—too many men looked like Salisbury—and Daintree didn't in any case want to spread the description just yet, especially to no avail: the M.P. was, he fancied, simply not in on this side of Esther Marko's activities. He looked down at the limp body on the floor. 'I'll send a man,' he said. 'Leave this to me.'

'No report to the local station?'

'No. And no talking about Esther Marko—to anyone. The man who comes won't ask questions. I repeat—no talking. Impress that on your wife.'

* * *

Before leaving the house, Daintree searched the body and took away the dead woman's handbag. He drove back to the Yard and set the wheels in motion: CID would not be involved at this stage, he preferred it kept within the Branch. The fullest secrecy would be observed and the body would be brought to a very special mortuary pending Daintree's further investigations. After two telephone calls had settled this, Daintree went through the handbag and struck gold. There were embassy identification, keys, lipstick, handkerchief, small engagement diary, money ... the usual clutter, but something else too—a photograph, showing a tallish man, big stomach, white hair, florid complexion, well-fed look, a nob. Daintree had his connection: the ratty man in Pentonville, Massey, Salisbury, Esther Marko, the Czech Embassy. Though the latter was in fact a doubtful one: Daintree believed Esther Marko had been working, as it were, outside her official status. That had seemed plain enough at their meeting. Nevertheless, the direction had opened up clear: Esther Marko had intended to communicate some information about Cunliffe, Delabier and Massey. True, she was now dead. But with any luck Salisbury wasn't.

Daintree did what he hadn't yet had the time to do, what with sundry interruptions: he rang Criminal Record Office and, in advance of sending down the photograph, passed the verbal description of Salisbury. He found the Commissioner had beaten him to it.

'Already checked,' CRO reported. 'Salisbury, blank. The description . . . *that* fits 500-odd files.'

'Your computers,' Daintree said bitterly, 'are wonderful!' He added, 'To confuse them further, I'm sending down a . . . no, I'm not after all.' He rang off, called another internal number and passed the 500 over to a superintendent for checking out: the Prime Minister had said, no stones . . . but Daintree had his other avenues that could prove faster and which might make better use of the photograph than CRO. Once more he used the phone, this time externally. When he got his man he said cryptically, 'Action park soonest possible,' and hung up.

* * *

Daintree walked through from the Yard to St James's Park. It was a beautiful morning: London looked clean and fresh though inevitably fume-hung from its traffic. The park was an oasis and plenty of people were refreshing themselves in its greenery, now turning autumn-tinted. Daintree, who kept a tin of bread crusts in his office, partly because it was useful cover and partly because he liked ducks anyway, hung over the rails of the bridge, thinking deeply about bridges without ducks . . . he broke his crusts and dropped the fragments, and the ducks swarmed, clucking and paddling with odd-shaped legs, beaks out-thrust in determination to be first. Fights ensued. Daintree looked down smiling. Ducks, even when fighting, spelled a kind of peace. Especially in the metal and concrete heart of London was this so. Daintree was almost beginning to relax when his man moved in: the same man he had met at Victoria some days before. He also carried crusts and looked as though he needed them more than the eager ducks. He broke and dropped, alongside Daintree.

'Lovely morning.'

'Yes, isn't it.'

'Queer things, ducks.'

'Very queer.'

They chatted, two strangers drawn together by an interest in ducks. Not to be hurried, despite that other bridge and its load of explosive, the ever-nearing shatter on the Forth. They hunched together, shoulder to shoulder, looking down with smiling faces. Then Daintree slid a hand into a pocket, held in his palm the photograph from Esther Marko's handbag. The man looked at it, his gaze taking it in on its way to the ducks. Daintree sweated: this man, unlikely as he appeared, was a compendium of crime, a connoisseur, a human computer of faces.

Daintree moved impatiently. 'Well?'

'I know him.'

A surge of blood, of excitement, rose in Daintree. 'Salisbury?'

'I beg your pardon?'

'You heard.'

'Yes, I did. Not Salisbury. Wrong diocese.' The man chuckled.

Daintree hissed, 'Oh, for God's sake—'

'Apologies, apologies.' More bread dropped, centring widening circles until snapped up. 'Eley. Joseph Eley.'

'Go on.'

'Rich. Stinking rich.'

'Doing what?'

'Oh—this and that, fiddles, rackets. Plays the Stock Exchange too. Never been caught up with by your chaps.' The thin man added reflectively, '*Nasty* bastard.'

'Address?'

'Down east, Poplar. Has an office . . . I don't know where his pad is—I think it changes pretty often. When I said fiddles . . . that provides the cream.'

'So he works?'

'Cover, just cover. Warehouse . . . import-export, about as busy as the grave. Better be careful, Daintree.' The man glanced at Daintree's set face, thoughtfully. 'Tell me, are you still on the same flog? You know what I mean.'

Daintree aimed a segment of crust at a duck's back. 'Yes. Is there a connection?'

'With Eley? I don't know.'

'Is Eley . . . Moscow-orientated?'

The man shrugged. 'I doubt it. Not really *involved*, I mean —as to his beliefs, ideals and so forth. Of course if it happened to suit him financially it'd be a different story.'

Daintree pondered. It was likely enough: a temporary allegiance, or alignment at any rate, in the name of profit. Cunliffe, Delabier and Massey to be—as he had once thought possible—virtually auctioned. He asked, 'Any other help forthcoming?'

'None. I'm sorry.'

'Positive?'

'Dead positive. If it was otherwise, I'd say. I don't like this either.'

Daintree sighed. 'You have the ring of truth. But God help you if you're holding out—*I* can be a bastard too, never mind Eley. Let's have the warehouse address.'

The man passed it. Daintree memorized it. Behind them, people passed—a copper, some soldiers, workmen with a ladder, hippies, well-dressed men, girls. From Wellington Barracks military music came, a march. Daintree said, 'Nice things, ducks.'

'On the greedy side . . .'

'Fade in three minutes, Piccadilly-wards. And keep your trap shut or I'll have you for treason.' Daintree left.

* * *

At RAF Hatherleigh, the aircraft waited still. Also still waiting were the troops from Colchester, but no longer were they in hiding. There was no more point in it. The press had smelled them out, and had broadcast their presence before Whitehall had had time to impose silence. Furious noises had issued from Downing Street, and certain editors stood currently in a certain degree of peril, but the damage had been done. The extent of it had become clear when, seen in the major's field-glasses, a man had emerged from the aircraft and had stood upon one of the wings, waving an arm around the perimeter in what was obviously mirthful greeting. He was too far off to be heard, but after a few moments he had gone back inside the aircraft to emerge again with a loud hailer, sounds from which came to the enditched soldiers in gusts, windblown.

'Good morning, Britishers. Our radio tells us you are there. We hope you are very comfortable. We play music to pass time for you. For now, cheerio.'

The man stayed on the wing, aiming his loud-hailer. *Colonel Bogey* came across, fitfully. More pertinently, orders were received from Colchester by radio: the troops were to remain guarding the perimeter and were not to communicate with the aircraft. They were not to move unless ordered, not to fire unless ordered. Frustrated, they emerged from their ditches and stood by their vehicles, listening to the music from the aircraft, feeling foolish.

* * *

On the Forth road bridge, in his fortressed isolation, Kahn also picked up the word that troops were in position around his spy-escape aircraft. As ever, he was unworried. 'Only to be expected,' he said with a shrug. 'They won't attack and they won't impede—and we all know why, don't we?'

He laughed.

He faced a silent audience: they were all in a bad way. The very atmosphere inside the coach—the lack of fresh air, the terrible cold fug behind the barred, closed windows, the smell of unwashed bodies, the personal feel of dirt on skin and clothing—it was all having its effect. Their limbs were cramped into an appalling restlessness that in many cases would not allow of sleep. Kahn would permit no exit from the coach at all now: even the emptying of the toilet bucket was performed by one of the armed men. Harkness, sitting behind his useless wheel as the sun crossed the great steel uprights that held the suspension cables of the bridge, casting shadows, had virtually given up hope. Surely, if the authorities were going to move, they would have moved by now? What were they doing? Kahn had allowed the hostages to hear the news bulletins but they gave no hope, no hope at all ... rather the reverse; the ball, they seemed to say, was in the hijackers' court now. They would not be given in to. They would be apprehended and duly punished: punishment could be avoided by surrender. The gist of the Prime Minister's answer to appeals made during the morning by deputations of Members of Parliament, the Trades Unions, and various women's organizations, was broadcast to the hijackers and their hostages: surrender would ensure free passage out of the country. Big concession! In the hearts of the trapped men and women, however, the unspoken inference was crystal clear: once the hostages were dead anyway, a mighty operation could be mounted with no more fear of reprisal. Gradually into those hearts settled a horrible conviction: they were being a nuisance to authority.

Harkness beat at his wheel in a frenzy of helpless misery.

* * *

Evening: short northern twilight on the bridge, with the sun a bright red circle sinking towards Glasgow and the Clyde, behind Bannockburn, ending its day-long climb from the Bass Rock. Lights flickered along the shore from houses and the occasional police or military vehicle moving its station. During the day, early in the day in fact, the crowds of rubbernecks had been cleared by police and soldiers who had dropped all politeness, men who would have liked nothing better than to use their weapons, use them on the gawping crowds. The searchlights played on Kahn's fortress again, from both bridge approaches and from the frigates below. Overhead, three helicopters hovered, the racket of their engines bringing no comfort at all. Aboard two of them, BBC and ITV cameramen recorded diligently; along the Forth were more Outside Broadcast cameras with long-distance lenses, mechanical ghouls exempt, in the sacred name of factual reporting, from police intervention. The sunset was a brilliant one: all the colours reaching in their glorious profusion across the sky, seeming to stretch into vast distances, with curious cloud formations like castles and mountains and glens... red, green, orange, purple. *Fearful lights that never beckon*, Harkness found himself murmuring aloud, thinking of the Northern Lights that he had seen on earlier, happier tours, *save when kings or heroes die....*

Into the evening's beauty came Rubery, seeking Kahn. 'Message coming through in the van,' he reported. His face was serious—scared, Harkness thought as he looked at him. Sudden hope leaped. Kahn went off with Rubery, leaving Silver and Kerrigan and another man on guard. Their footsteps died away along the bridge. There was something up—Harkness felt sure of it, something had gone wrong, though he scarcely dared to hope too much, to tempt fate into giving them all a slap in the face.

In the van Kahn spoke to the radioman.

'Well, what is it?'

'Makins.'

Makins was the London contact, the man in Church Street, Kensington. Kahn took over the set, called Makins. He said, 'Leader. Over.'

Just two words: 'Birds flown.'

Kahn's face was livid. 'Where and who?'

'I don't know where. Who, you can guess.'

'You're sure of this?'

'Positive.'

Kahn swore. The London man asked, 'So what do we do?'

Kahn stared out of the back doors of the big van, stared across the Forth, along the bridge towards the southern approaches. After a while he said in a dead flat voice, 'We get out. Inform Hatherleigh, take-off soonest possible. Inform Saviour, operation midnight precisely. And inform Whitehall, deadline midnight. They have till then to find the birds. Out.'

No arguments on the air: but in the van, dissention. Rubery was unhappy. 'How sure is Makins?' he asked.

'Makins is reliable. I take his word—and we all know who was likely to try to cut us out. Those bastards won't be showing.' Kahn's eyes were red slits. 'For now—just for now—it looks like we've had it.'

'But the government assurance—the free pardon—'

'If you believe that,' Kahn said through his teeth, 'you'll believe anything. We're getting out as planned. Once we're out of Britain... we'll hook them back. And the coach and the bridge will blow as soon as we're clear away.' Turning, he went back to the coach and called for Silver. Silver moved up the gangway.

'Yes?'

Kahn, his face devilish in the glare from the probing searchlights, said, 'Fix the primers, then set up the transmitter inside the coach. After that, lock and evacuate.' He raised his voice, addressing the hostages. 'Anyone who tries anything, dies now. Deadline midnight.'

There was a shocked silence. Then Elsie Peach started crying. Harkness looked at his watch: 18.35.

16

LEAVING St James's Park, Daintree had checked with CRO: nothing known of Joseph Eley. He was listed in the Directory of Directors as chairman and managing director of an import-export agency in the City, with warehouse accommodation in Poplar. The City address was that of an accountant—the company's registered address. Daintree made his dispositions, losing no time. He brought in Crime now, with the fullest approval of the Commissioner and the Assistant Commissioner Crime: he was given permission to call upon any regional crime squad he might find necessary. Acting as co-ordinator, he made the initial penetration himself, alone, backed at a distance by hand-picked plain-clothes men from the Branch and from CID, with cars stationed in handy but discreet spots on a wide perimeter around Joseph Eley's warehouse.

Later in the morning rain had come, suddenly and surprisingly, to dim London's day: Daintree went in dressed nondescriptly in an old mackintosh, his hair glistening with water. Eley's Poplar warehouse was not far from the old West India Dock. There was a river smell, a hint of mist, a hint of deep waters and seaborne trade, nostalgic of a lost Empire. In the warehouse a vague, faint reminder of Eastern spices: but in fact the warehouse was empty but for one pile of crates, isolated in the middle of a vast floor-space. There was no-one about. There were several heavy doors, painted grey. One of them, a big one, looked like a way for bulky freight, probably to and from the river. Daintree's footsteps echoed from high, dirty walls.

He found a wooden staircase in one corner, and he climbed it, creakily, towards a landing, off which opened a frosted-glass-paned door bearing the one black-painted word:

OFFICE. Daintree knocked: no answer. He turned the handle, and went in. He entered a sort of lobby, dirty faded green with a bare board floor. There was, oddly, a smell of kippers. Off the lobby, three more doors opened. One was labelled, once again, OFFICE. Another, GENERAL OFFICE. The third was the lavatory, unsexed. Probably only men worked here anyway. In the room marked OFFICE an electric light burned, and Daintree knocked and went in without waiting. From behind a paper-littered deal table a man looked up. Not Salisbury—not Eley but a bent old man in shirt-sleeves, wearing one of those green eye-shades once beloved of newspaper editors in ancient films. The air was hot: in one corner a smelly gas-stove burned dangerously.

'Good morning,' the old man said, coughing.

'Good morning. Mr Eley?'

'Not in, I'm sorry. Can I help?'

'I doubt it, it's Mr Eley I wanted. I can wait.'

'It'll be a long wait. He's away on holiday.'

'Oh, dear.' Daintree looked sad. 'Where's he gone?'

'Continent, France. South of. Lovely weather.' The old man looked envious, downtrodden, a workhorse. Genuine, or a good actor? 'Who might *you* be, if I may ask?'

'Name of Foster.'

'Foster...' The old clerk searched his memory, frowning.

'You won't know me. I met Joe Eley once,' Daintree said. 'Thought I might put a bit of business his way... know what I mean?'

'Maybe I do, maybe I don't. I don't discuss Mr Eley's business, Mr Foster.'

'No? Well, you're right, of course. I was wondering—since he's not here—if you'd be kind enough to give me his home address? He's not in the telephone—'

'Ex-directory,' the man said, coughing again. His face seemed to have closed up suddenly. 'Why not come back another day? If he's in the south of France, he won't be at home, will he, so what's the use?'

Daintree shrugged. 'Little enough, except that I'm a busy man and I could ring him at home after he's back.'

No answer: Daintree's mind rooted through the chances.

This old man wasn't communicative, and that could be natural: he could be, simply, loyal—old-fashioned, but then he was an old man. On the other hand, it could be self-interest ... on the wall hung a clock with a dirty, cracked face. Daintree's eye was drawn to it, inexorably: 12.15. Time was short, was important—was vital. Time shouted for chances to be taken, for quick decisions in the interest of a number of human lives.

Daintree asked casually, 'Those crates in the warehouse. What's in them?'

'Machine parts. I—'

'Where for—or where from, perhaps?'

'Read, can't you?'

'They happened,' Daintree said smoothly, 'to be blank.'

'Oh—yes!' A slip, hastily to be covered? 'Christ, I forgot. Haven't been stencilled yet. But what's it to you?'

Daintree plunged. 'My name is Daintree. I'm a senior officer of the Special Branch. Your name?'

'Mellor.' The old clerk didn't seem especially worried.

'Right, Mr Mellor. I want those crates opened up, at once, please.'

'Just as you like,' the old man said, smiling. 'You'll be accountable afterwards to Mr Eley, of course.' He got to his feet.

* * *

It took time—time and a couple of crowbars, wielded by Mellor and by Daintree himself. Machine parts spilled out in profusion—small stuff mainly. Certainly no room for Cunliffe, Delabier or Massey. Daintree scowled: perhaps it had been too melodramatic in any case, but similar stowages had been used from time to time in his experience. Holding the old man by the arm, he used his two-way radio: in fast response, a plain-clothes man sauntered in from the street. Daintree indicated his prisoner. 'Name of Mellor. I'm holding him for questioning,' he said. 'Take him back to the Yard. Helping the police with their enquiries.'

'Look here,' Mellor said.

'Looking. Have you anything to tell me?'

'Like bloody hell! What is there to tell?'

Daintree smiled. 'That, we'll be finding out. Do you know anything about Cunliffe, Delabier and Massey?'

'*That* lot?' Mellor stared wide-eyed. 'Course I don't... only what I've heard on the telly and read in the papers!' He gave a creaky laugh that ended in a fit of coughing. 'Think they was here, did you?'

'Never mind what I thought,' Daintree said gruffly. 'If you decide to talk about Joseph Eley, you may save yourself a lot of unpleasantness.' He waited. 'No?'

'No.'

Daintree made a sign to the plain-clothes man. 'All right, take him away. And I want this place sealed off, then gone through with a toothcomb.'

He went back up to the office. There, a telephone stood. If he waited, it might ring. The caller might, given time, be Joseph Eley alias Salisbury. Daintree left the office again, went down to the warehouse, out into the street and into a telephone box. He dialled the Yard, and gave the office number. 'I want a tap put on the line. And I want all conversations to be taped.' He went back, across the warehouse where his men were busy sounding walls and floors and investigating what lay behind the various doors. Back in the office suite, if it could be called that, Daintree joined other men going through desks and cupboards in the otherwise deserted General Office: also in the old managing clerk's room. They didn't find anything that helped, just old files, and documents relating to current business—it all, at first sight anyway, looked genuine. This done, Daintree sat hunched in the chair vacated by Mellor. He lit a cigarette, smoked it quickly to a stub and lit another before it expired. His nerves were playing him up. Always, you had to balance one thing against another: he could be wasting that valuable, shortening time and he knew it, feeling sick with the knowledge. But he saw no alternative: the lead to Eley was not only good, but it was all he had.

At 13.45 the telephone rang, startling Daintree. He answered. It was a girl's voice—a young girl, efficient-secretary type. 'Is that Ffoulkes-Fordyce Import?'

'Speaking.'

A pause. 'Mr Mellor?'

The old clerk. 'He's gone off for lunch... and got the afternoon off too.' The girl thanked him, said it didn't matter, Mr somebody or other wanted to know about a shipment, but maybe she would call back later. She didn't. Daintree, a man of insight, knew she wasn't anything more than a genuine customer, if that was the word in import-export. Though she wouldn't know it, she was now down for posterity, on tape. The telephone remained silent thereafter: like the man in the park had said, not a busy warehouse. At 15.33 a plain-clothes man came up from the warehouse. Daintree said, 'You've been a long time.'

'A lot to go through, sir. There's outbuildings, and a sizeable yard going down to the river—'

'So I saw from the window—'

'And a wharf, sir.'

'Find anything?' Daintree asked, sounding gloomy.

'Not a thing, sir. Just—well, junk really.'

'They don't seem to be busy, do they? I wonder why! I'll tell you something: it's a lovely place for getting men out of the country, Pullen. Built for it.'

'Well, maybe, sir. But they wouldn't get them far, not before they're searched.'

Daintree said, still gloomy, 'I wouldn't bank on it. The river police are bloody good, but this lot's playing high. Well, we can but wait. That's all.'

The plain-clothes man hesitated, looking worried. 'What do you think is going to happen?' he asked.

Daintree said, shrugging, 'It's just a hunch, but I've a feeling—and it's a strong one—that we're due for a general gaol delivery... if you get me! Cunliffe, Delabier and Massey for export.'

'When, sir?'

'Any bloody time, Pullen, any bloody time at all.' He added, 'Now the toothcomb is over, I want your men kept in cover. Good cover, all right?'

Pullen said, 'Nobody'll see a thing, sir.'

* * *

At 18.50 hours, with Daintree still waiting by the telephone and with darkness settling over the warehouse and its wharf in Poplar a shatter of sound reached the troops on watch around the Hatherleigh perimeter: the running-up of aircraft engines.

The major, reacting fast, reported by radio and then obeyed high-level orders already received. Troops streamed across the old airfield towards the runway: too late. The great dark machine, no lights burning, came into wind and roared down the concrete, swaying as the wheels bumped over the irregularities. Faster and faster... gaining airspeed, it lifted, wheels folding neatly into the belly. Some of the troops, within range now, fired blind but did no apparent damage. Up into the sky and away, turning easterly, back for the coast and the silent grey waste of the North Sea, out of reach of the military might of Colchester....

The next order came from the Defence Ministry and was addressed to RAF Wyton: 'Shadow closely but do not, repeat not bring down. Safety of hostages now paramount.'

* * *

The telephone line to the warehouse was not to be used from the Yard: the message reached Daintree via his pocket radio, on his personal call sign: 'Aircraft gone, is being shadowed.'

Daintree, not acknowledging for security reasons, flicked off the radio and stood wondering. Surrender? Or some fresh trick? Kahn in the coach was not supposed to know about Cunliffe, Delabier and Massey—but did he? Or was this all a blind, were the spies being got out by other means but still into the hands of Kahn and his associates?

Irresolution settled, an appalling irresolution that took Daintree by the throat and for a while inhibited constructive thought. Then, on the heels of the first, the second radio message came in, the sender's voice sounding strained and high, unnatural beyond all radio-transmission unnaturalness: 'Broadcast picked up, pinpointed Kensington area north of High Street, refers to a message from Forth road bridge. Disappearance of spies known to hijackers. *Deadline midnight, repeat deadline midnight.'*

Daintree's hands trembled as he looked at his wrist-watch. Under five hours to go. That message—the sender, known to be somewhere north of High Street, Kensington: a biggish area, but a search was clearly vital and it had to be in time. Daintree sweated, havered, decided to remain where he was. The Commissioner would be coping with the rest. Daintree, however, knew it was unlikely he would find anything: the moment that message had been passed, Kensington would be clear of villains. To identify them on the run would be next to impossible. Sweating, biting his nails to the quick, Daintree sat in the office, in the dark, waiting, praying as he had never prayed before.

* * *

Down below in the warehouse Pullen also waited, hidden behind the re-stowed crates of machine parts. Others waited with him, keeping dead still and quiet, guns ready: they were all marksmen. They were all experienced officers: even their breathing, that night, would not have upset a marauding mouse. Like Daintree they waited in darkness, listened to the splash of rain outside: Poplar was enduring a downpour. Suddenly, startlingly at precisely 21.37 hours, they heard the distant ring of Daintree's telephone. Up in the office Daintree felt the increased thump of his heart like an embodied drum. He reached for the telephone.

A voice—an educated voice, slightly plummy—came to him: 'All okay, Mellor?'

Daintree masked the mouthpiece with a hand and spoke with an old, old voice covered by a nasty cough. 'Yes.'

'Rendezvous as planned, then.'

The call was cut.

Daintree slammed down the handset and ran out of the office, thundered down the wooden steps, using a torch, calling for Pullen. Pullen emerged from his crates. 'Sir?'

'It won't be here. It won't be here, but stand by right where you are for orders. I'll be back.' Daintree raced out into the street, into the soaking downpour. Saturated, he made the telephone box he had used earlier in the day. Inside was a couple, doing almost everything but make a telephone call. Daintree yanked the door open. 'Out!' he said.

'Christ, you—'

Daintree brought out his automatic. 'Get!'

With a terrified shriek from the girl, they got. Daintree went in and dialled an emergency private number at the Yard. He said, 'Daintree. For the Commissioner himself, bloody fast: squeeze Mellor, squeeze him dry. This is vital enough to use every method known to man and beast. Tell the Commissioner just that. And tell him, I'm on my way in.'

17

MELLOR was tougher by far than he looked. Senior Yard officers had started the grill minutes after Daintree had called in, but Mellor wasn't saying a thing. Daintree had a private word with the Commissioner, after hearing the nil report regarding Mellor.

He gave the Commissioner the brief details of the phone-call to the warehouse. He said, 'For my money, sir, the rendezvous involves Cunliffe, Delabier and Massey, all set for out. And Mellor knows where that rendezvous is to be.' His eyes blazed feverishly. 'We have to make him cough. We have to!'

'You've no idea—in a broad sense—where the rendezvous might be?'

'None, sir. I've only that phone-call to go on, nothing else. Well?'

The Commissioner met his eye: both men knew what was being suggested. In Daintree's view, the situation had moved beyond the decencies of life, beyond the correct official formulae of interrogation. Mellor was of less importance than the lives at stake on the Forth road bridge: it had become a question of priorities. Daintree knew he had to act fast now on his own initiative and take on a huge personal responsibility, and at the same time, in the doing of it, lie. He said, 'Just leave it to me, sir. It will be done properly, by the book.' To himself he added, *my book*.

He had spoken to the Commissioner in the passage outside the room where Mellor was being held. Without saying more, he turned away and went into the room: it was bare, austere, the paintwork clean but scuffed. Mellor sat at a plain table, facing Daintree's man, a senior officer of the Branch, with a CID officer taking notes. On the door, a constable. Daintree sent them all outside, and sat on the table close to Mellor, looking down at him.

'Now,' he said. 'Now, you bastard, you're going to talk.'

* * *

On the Forth, the drama was unfolding into the final act, a drama in the full glare of footlights, nationwide. Down the length of Britain, and overseas, people waited: the television screens had shown the coach in the searchlights, and the waiting, inactive troops at each end of the bridge: the news broadcasts would in due time tell all. It was as though the whole country held its breath and kept its fingers crossed. In many homes it was agonizingly personal: perhaps most of all in Peckham where driver Harkness lived. Harkness was the only one with young dependent children—the only other children so involved were the two youngsters themselves in Kahn's grip, the youngsters who had now been taken to the headquarters van. Harkness had many friends: they spoke of him that night, as they had so often spoken these last few days, in the pubs. In his own local, it was almost a graveyard watch, with the television showing what in effect was the coffin to be. The 21.00 news broadcast had told the world of the new deadline; but secrecy was being maintained still as to the disappearance of the three spies, the combined cause of all the trouble. As a result, the name of the government stank: they, and they alone seemingly, had the means to resolve it all, but they, the hard-faced powerful men, were taking no action.

In the coach, they were now sealed off behind their barred windows, behind the locked doors—very securely sealed from the outside. Harkness had wound down the windows to clear the fug, had touched the unyielding steel of Silver's welded bars, had battered at it with his bare hands in a sudden frenzy of fear. They had watched the transmitter being set up inside the coach, ready to send their pleas to the world beyond the bridge. They had heard Silver busy in the boot, priming the charges that would fragment them. Kahn and the others had now withdrawn to one of the removal vans. The passengers could see the thin trails of the fuses leading along the carriageway of the bridge, into the van, ready for ignition. Six minutes, Kahn had said. They would be able to count the seconds once they saw the first red spark of fire. In those six minutes, clearly, Kahn and his hijackers would be getting out. Surely, then, they—the hijackers—would be open to attack? There could be no excuse for giving them free passage, *not then*, when the coach and the bridge would be all set to blow within minutes?

Harkness found his brain racing along that track: somewhere, something was wrong—it had to be. Kahn couldn't have slipped into a stupid error: whatever his degree of confidence hitherto, he must know now that he couldn't get away? Of course, he had spoken of another method of detonation: remote control by radio. But in that case, why the fuse trail?

Why?

Harkness worried around the point. Worrying, getting nowhere, he half listened to the sounds from outside, was visually aware of all that was going on in their vicinity. Helicopters, high-flying aircraft crossing and re-crossing, the brilliant searchlights, four ships below them now—the two frigates plus two smaller craft, also with searchlights and guns. Beyond the blocking removal vans, north and south, the police and troops had closed in further, were now within twenty or thirty yards of the barbed-wire barricades. Harkness thought bitterly: *and all so bloody useless!*

Unable now to sit still, tormented by his nagging thoughts, he got up and looked down the gangway crowded with the people from the trapped cars. Neck craning, Harkness tried to seek out General Pendennis but couldn't find him. Then he remembered. Along with those two children from the dormobile, Pendennis had been removed by Kahn before the coach had been sealed and taken to Kahn's headquarters van.

Harkness felt blood rush to his head: God, but he'd been bloody slow! One VIP, two kids—Kahn's safe-conduct out. And the fuse trail... that was what would finish them off, not—now—the remote control device. That had been intended only for the later cover of Kahn's escape, and the safety of the aircraft from Hatherleigh. It would presumably have been used only if the fuse itself had not been lit—if the authorities in Whitehall had agreed to a handover.

Which, clearly now, they had not and would not.

To Harkness, as he stood there looking down the coach, it was the final end of hope.

* * *

'It's only a foretaste,' Daintree said. 'When you go inside, Mellor, having let around forty people die in Scotland, the cons aren't going to like you. I'd ponder on that, if I were you.'

Mellor bled from the nose and from one cut eye. He sniffled.

'You'll have—what? Thirty years, perhaps more, for pondering. I hope you enjoy it—and your conscience, if you've any.' Daintree, standing in his shirt sleeves now, reached out for Mellor's head and rattled it. A top set of dentures came loose. A clout on the side of the head ejected them: Daintree ground them beneath a foot. He slapped the face hard so that it jerked from side to side like a doll's. Mellor cried, and tears mixed with blood, drooled down to his collar. He was a mess.

'I can keep this up for hours,' Daintree said. Slap, slap, slap. 'Talk, Mellor, and it'll stop. I'll put in a word for you . . . you helped the police. You saved the people in the coach. You could almost be a kind of hero. All you have to do is say where the rendezvous is.'

Mellor didn't cough. Daintree looked at his watch: half an hour wasted—fifty minutes, since he'd made his phone-call from near the warehouse. Too long: now, there was under two hours to go, it was bloody impossible. Daintree shook as with a fever: he wanted to kill Mellor. If it hadn't been so useless, he felt he would have done. But through crazed rage and frustration he made a decision. He went to the door, yanked it open, faced the guarding officers.

'Watch Mellor,' he said. 'Clean him up. Tell the Commissioner, I'm going back to Eley's place.'

* * *

The Prime Minister was on the line to the Home Secretary. 'Is there any news?'

'None, sir.' The Home Secretary's hand smoothed the expensive leather of his desk.

'Where's that man Daintree?'

'On his way back to the Poplar warehouse, Prime Minister, after interrogating his suspect, a fruitless interrogation.'

'There's not long to go.'

'No...'

The Prime Minister said, 'I've a crowd outside in the street.' He sounded highly nervous. 'They're getting out of hand, I think.'

'So I'm told. I've already spoken to Scotland Yard. There'll be more men with you soon, sir. As a matter of fact...'

'Yes?'

'There's a certain amount of racket in Whitehall.' A little earlier the Home Secretary had had his windows shut: shouts, obscenities, threats, clashes with police didn't tend to help nerves already on edge. Things were getting nasty. He said, 'Prime Minister, I fancy there will be real trouble unless we lift the security—let it be known to the public, there's no current availability of Cunliffe, Delabier and—'

'It's too late for that! Too late for it to spread effectively.' The voice was rattled, panicky now. 'I want contact made with the Forth road bridge. I think you'd better talk personally to the terrorists.'

'Saying what?'

'Ask them to hold off. We're doing our best to get those three back. Tell them that. And tell them... when we're successful, a handover will be considered.'

The Home Secretary gaped. 'But—'

'Please do just as I say. We don't want—bloodshed. I say again, the crowd is nasty.'

The call was cut. The Home Secretary looked up at his Permanent Under-Secretary. He said the one word: 'Surrender.'

Pursed lips responded: 'Unwise, very! A precedent....'

'He's rattled. He scents the mob.' Giving point to his

words, the window-muted sounds from Whitehall grew louder, penetrating the room's brooding, mahogany opulence.

The Permanent Under-Secretary smiled thinly. 'Oh, come, there won't be much of a reaction in the event, you know that. We British... there'll be noises off, like now, no more than that. He's funking the issue, in my opinion.' The official Civil Service view had been stated, primly. 'I consider this a bad decision.'

'It's not quite a decision yet, but if it comes we must obey.'

Wheels were set in motion: the contact was made as ordered. Five minutes after that contact, Kahn was back on the air with his reply: deadline extended two hours, and that was final. Delivery to the bridge on recapture.

The Prime Minister, his face white as he listened to the clamour in Downing Street, was informed accordingly.

* * *

Daintree's progress back to Poplar had been fast but unheralded by flashing blue lights or other impedimenta to secrecy. Out of sight from the warehouse, he sent his car away with a plain-clothes driver. Walking on, he went into the warehouse, stopped, listened. Light from a street lamp illuminated him, cast his shadow into the silent warehouse. He heard a voice—Pullen's: 'Over here, sir.'

Briefly, a torch flashed. Daintree moved for the crates, got into cover. 'All quiet?'

'All very quiet, sir, no visitors. The phone rang—'

'I fancied it might,' Daintree said with satisfaction. 'You didn't answer, I hope?'

'No, sir. And glad I did right! Why are you back, sir?'

'No joy from Mellor. But it occurred to me that when he didn't make the rendezvous, they might well call him again. Also, that when the phone remained unanswered, they just might come along to find out why. Just might, Pullen.'

There was a quiet laugh. 'Good thinking, sir! And if they do?'

Daintree said, 'We watch. We listen. And, as ever, we bloody well pray. But we don't start anything till I say. Pass the word, please.'

Quietly, like a shadow, Pullen did so. Then they just waited, as motionless as men could be, listening, watching. Once again, the telephone rang, up in the office, urgent, insistent, but unanswered. When it stopped, the silence was twice as intense. No sound from the river, rolling past only yards away, no lap of water even: the ebb had set in some time previously, and only dirty mud now connected with the old grimed stone of the wharf outside. Occasionally through the dirty, cracked glass of windows set high in the river wall, a strong light sent shadows chasing weirdly across the ceiling: the launches of Thames Division, the river police patrolling their water-beat. Now and again there was the scurry of a rat.

Nothing else.

Daintree came out in a cold sweat as he looked, time and again, at his watch.

* * *

'We're not doing any good moping,' Harkness said suddenly. 'Let's think of the ... good things, eh?' It sounded silly and he knew it, but it was the best he could do. If they were soon to go out like lights along a summer promenade, he thought, it was dreadful to be like this at the last. 'Think of what they're doing for us, outside there. We're not forgotten, you know.'

They stared back at him, dully, like so many dummies, he thought with sudden irrational anger—no-hopers, with no reaction left. They had composed themselves to die, but good God, he thought, we haven't gone yet! He forced a smile, hoped it looked cheery but knew it looked ghastly behind his stubble of beard, like the grin on a skeleton. He said, 'Once—not so long ago—we *sang*. Eh, Miss MacBean? So how about us doing it again?'

No response.

Harkness cleared his throat, felt a terrible and mounting sensation of naked dread like a knife in the guts, knew he had to dispel it for himself and all the others or they would go out in a pusillanimous panic. He began to sing, the first tune that came into his mind on the wings of his fear.

> It's a long way to Tipperary,
> It's a long way to go...

Still no response, and Harkness let his voice trail away, tried to keep smiling. In the gangway the father from the dormobile started shouting, the first real sign of the end. 'God... I can't take it, I can't take it! Let me get out.' He began fighting through towards the front, towards the fast-bolted doors to freedom, over the heads of the waiting frigates from the Rosyth command. Tears streamed down his face. The American, MacFee, barred his way and let him have it, right on the point of the jaw. For now, panic was halted, but it would come back, Harkness knew. He watched MacFee: the American was rubbing his fist, looking sorry for what he had had to do, his face and voice gentle. He said, 'Well, I guess our driver's right. We got to keep bright. Now, won't you all try singing with Mr Harkness and me?'

He opened his mouth, but he was beaten to it. Miss MacBean the elder got to her feet near the middle of the coach, indomitably Scottish. Harkness had a premonition that Auld Lang Syne was coming... he felt a lump rise in his throat as he looked at Miss MacBean, her head and her colour high, her shoulders square like a highlander of old, like the man on the Black Watch memorial in Aberfeldy where first the singing had started.

But it was not Auld Lang Syne that she had in mind. She said in a loud, strong voice, 'Listen, all of you. Our grandfather went down in the *Titanic*. They didn't face death without some spirit in those days! My sister and I hope you'll all join in. Now.'

The two MacBeans started.

> Abide with me. Fast falls the eventide...

Harkness was weeping openly. He slid a hand towards the transmitter left by Kahn, switching it on. Maybe when this reached London, somebody would relent.

18

IN THE warehouse, Daintree thought at first it was just another rat making its scurrying corner-noises. So did Pullen. But the next noise was a creak—it came suddenly and as suddenly stopped, to be followed by silence.

Daintree, close to Pullen, whispered into his ear, 'Rats don't open doors.'

'Action?'

'Not yet.'

They waited, not making a sound. The creak, after what seemed a long time, came again: unmistakably, one of the doors leading off to their right. The big cargo-door to the wharf? Very likely—certainly, in fact. Whoever was coming, would have come from the river. Now there was a very faint loom of river-light, more creaking, and then footsteps. The footsteps crossed the floor of the warehouse and then were heard ascending the wooden stairway to the office. Daintree heard the door at the top being opened, felt a nudge from Pullen, who asked, 'Do we go in now, sir?'

'No. Maybe he wants to use the phone.'

'Do we let him?'

In the darkness, Daintree grinned. 'Why not? Why not let him say it's all quiet here ... if he wants to?'

They listened as they waited, ears straining, but they couldn't catch the single ding of a lifted receiver. In any case the man wasn't up there long. They heard him coming down the stairway, and this time they saw his movement too because he was using a torch. Daintree could not distinguish the man himself behind the beam but had already judged him, from the footfalls, to be big-built: the wooden steps were taking punishment. Daintree waited still: He decided not to show for the moment.

Someone else, however, did show.

There was a movement over by the door from the street, the door which Daintree, on re-entering, had taken care to shut but had not bolted. The door opened and another torch beamed in. In the street light, Daintree saw the familiar helmet. A beat-patrolling copper, a foot man, nosing as was his duty. Daintree softly cursed. At the bottom of the stairway now, the unknown, big-built man halted.

The copper's torch shone out, showing him up. Daintree stiffened. Big, yes—and with white hair, and a belly, and a pink face: *Joseph Eley!* Gold had been struck. Daintree damned the copper, damned also his own lurking, hidden outposts for not having intercepted the copper's prowl. But still he waited.

The copper spoke. 'What's your business, sir?'

'My business?' The voice was very English, just as the ratty man in Pentonville had said. Clipped, authoritative, unaccented. 'Look around you!'

'I mean,' the policeman explained, 'what are you doing here now, at this time of night?'

'It's my warehouse.' There was a laugh. 'I suppose you found the door open?'

'Unlocked, sir, yes. May I ask your name?'

'Eley. Joseph Eley.'

The constable remained silent. Daintree, his heart in his mouth now, tried to assess, to see into the copper's mind. Cunliffe, Delabier and Massey must of a certainty be on this constable's personal list. But he wouldn't necessarily be thinking in terms of warehouses in Poplar. And Joseph Eley would not be on his list: Eley was Daintree's own property, the concern of Special Branch alone, the experts in the field, and CID had been informed accordingly. Joseph Eley, however, would be in a mood to take no chances at this stage. Daintree felt suddenly very cold: because of himself, because of his methods of handling, a young constable might be about to die. Somewhere down the chain of command, and it could have originated with himself, there had been a slip. The beat men should have been warned off this area and they hadn't been. Daintree reached into a pocket and brought out his cigarette lighter.

He threw it hard, towards his right, away from the constable, away from Eley. It hit the wall with a small clatter, enough to bring Eley round on his heel, turning from the constable—enough to make Eley show his hand. Just in time, that copper saw the gun that came out, and just in time he acted. He threw himself on Eley, bringing him to the ground, and Daintree flicked on his own torch and shouted an order. In seconds a battery of police automatics stared down at Eley. The pink face was a dangerous red.

'Get up,' Daintree said. He jerked his gun. 'Quick!'

Eley got up, chest heaving, eyes watchful.

'Where have you come from?'

No answer.

'Where are Cunliffe, Delabier and Massey?'

Daintree heard the gasp from the nosing copper. He turned to him. 'Commander Daintree, Special Branch. You can relax. Search this man.'

'Yes, sir.' Quickly, the copper ran his hands over Eley's body: no more weapons. He opened the jacket, went through the pockets. Like Esther Marko's handbag, Daintree watched the emergence of the usual collection, wallet included. No help —not unexpectedly. There was no time to try to make Joseph Eley talk: Daintree's watch showed 23.05. Daintree poured sweat: fifty-five minutes left to produce three spies. It was ridiculous, just a recovery operation from now on: much too late to save the people on the bridge. Daintree spoke to Pullen. 'Get round him,' he said harshly. 'Any trouble, don't hesitate, immobilize him, don't kill him. The kneecaps should do it.' He tried just once. Addressing Eley he asked, 'Want to save yourself some trouble?'

Eley said, 'I don't know what you're talking about.'

'Then you'll soon be a lot wiser.' Daintree gestured to Pullen as his officers moved in around Eley in a close ring, with guns. 'Come on—with me, all of you. We're going outside, the way *he* came in.'

He went fast for the door. Behind him came Eley. Daintree had no idea of the next step, but expected to find a boat of some sort: Eley, he felt sure, must have come in from the river itself rather than a cloak-and-dagger clamber over high walls to bypass the main entry. His neat clothing, for one thing, hadn't the clamber look. Outside, Daintree swung his torch. No-one about, just a cat on the roof of a store, licking its fur, a cat that broke off licking when it heard Daintree, and arched its back, and spat. Daintree's torch beam travelled along the wharf, over the side, down to the dark river, low-water-distant. Mud and rubble, no boat at the water's edge. Daintree, baffled, turned on Eley. He waved an arm, upstream. 'Once, somewhere along there, they used to peg out pirates at low water. When the tide came in, they drowned. Like rats. I can do the same to you, Joseph Eley.'

He meant it—right then, he meant it. Inspector Pullen knew he meant it, and gasped: in the 1970's, you couldn't. Daintree felt the blood rise, felt that his head would burst. Lights danced in his brain, jagged electric flickers. He was about to give the order, see what it would achieve, when he was saved. The uniformed constable, who was not one of the Eley-guarding ring, had wandered, using his torch. He called out suddenly.

Daintree swung round. 'Yes?'

'Over here, sir.'

Daintree moved towards the light, conscious as he started that Eley had reacted. There was a new look in the eyes, and a kind of whiteness to fade the pink. Daintree picked his way past clutter—ring-bolts for moorings, old tin cans, lengths of chain handy for securing Eley in a pirate's, or a traitor's, slow-motion grave. Reaching the constable, he asked, 'Well?'

'Down there, sir.' The torch beamed out over an inlet channel to the inner basin, showing the knuckle of the wharf: with the ebb, the river had left the channel dry outwards of a lock gate, fast shut to hold the water in the basin. 'See it, sir?'

Daintree looked. The white beam had steadied on the farther side of the entry channel, on the solid dirty stone of the wharf wall. A rusty iron door, very heavy, with great rusted hinges, was set in the stone three feet up from the river bed.

'Traces of oil, sir, on the hinges.'

'And rubber insulation . . . watertight.' Daintree put a hand on the constable's shoulder. 'Well done! A secret strong-room?'

'Or a tunnel, sir. A tunnel under the river—one that the man Eley came through?'

Daintree sucked in breath. 'Possible.' He felt a great excitement, a virtual certainty that more than gold had now been struck. 'Did you *know* of a tunnel?'

'No, sir. I'm new on this beat—*any* beat, sir.'

'Read your literature, laddie. It'll be mapped for sure. All the same, I'm grateful.' He turned, called. 'Inspector Pullen, over here. All of you.'

The torches moved towards him, stopped. Daintree didn't bother to question Joseph Eley. He made his dispositions. 'This constable and two plain-clothes men to stay in cover here on the wharf. Two others, down by the iron door. Another in the warehouse—and he's first to contact the men and mobiles in reserve. They're to remain in cover and watch the road outside. The rest, plus Eley, come with me. Just one moment.' He brought out his two-way radio, and flicked it on. 'CSB4 to base. Red alert, repeat red alert, area immediately opposite.'

Flicking off again, he nodded at Pullen. 'Right,' he said.

* * *

In the operations room at the Yard, down the long line of uniformed officers at telephones and transceivers, the men who listened in constantly to the crime heart-beat of London, there was, when Daintree's message came in, as much of a silence as was ever possible. The message arrived along with the trivialities; lost dogs, nicked cars, reports of obscene telephone calls, dropped keys, all manner of items that panic reactions said warranted a 999 call. Daintree's message, specially monitored, was reported within seconds to the Commissioner, present in person with his deputy and the ACC. Daintree's area being known, 'opposite' meant Rotherhithe and the Surrey Commercial Docks across the river. To this area went many mobiles carrying a strong force. At the same time a fresh alert, and fresh information with it, was passed to Thames Division, whose river launches began to swing for convergence on Limehouse Reach.

* * *

Down on the river bed, feet crunching on stones, mud, weed and broken bottles, nose assailed by the low-water smell of the river, Daintree reached for the rusted iron door and its heavy securing bar, the end of which slotted into a socket in a thick iron stanchion riveted to the stonework.

He gave the bar a sharp pull and it came clear with no trouble. He glanced briefly at Eley: Eley, who had no doubt felt secure enough not to bother with locking the door behind himself. He said, 'In—Eley first, but hang on to him.' Daintree swung the door open like an oven. There was a sucking sensation as he did so. Blackness yawned, a dark pit of God knew what. The opening was a good two feet square, not hard to hoist oneself into. Urged by strong arms, Eley went up, with an officer gripping the waistband of his trousers at the back and another holding tight to a foot. Next in line, Daintree went up: his arrival just about filled the available space inside the door. Raising his head cautiously as he beamed his torch ahead, Daintree found room to stand—just, with bent shoulders. They were in a square cavern, and ahead the way ran down a steep slope into which rough steps had been cut. The construction was of stone and the smell was river-dank, and from far ahead there came a sound of dripping as the Thames penetrated. Daintree shivered, looked round. 'Down the steps,' he said, his voice sounding strangely flat, with no carrying quality—he would have expected some sort of echo. 'Take it slow, take it carefully, and keep Eley in front.'

They moved down the steps, doing their best to keep their feet on slippery stone. As they cleared the entry chamber, the other plain-clothes men came up and in behind. The dank smell increased as they penetrated the tunnel and as the iron door was pulled shut behind the last man to enter.

On slowly. They reached the bottom of the steps, went on along a shallow down-slope. Nothing happened, no sound was heard apart from the water-drip. River water descended through bed-mud and old brick and dripped down the back of Daintree's collar. The torches were off now: they advanced by feel alone—hands and feet, the latter ready for some sudden drop. They went silently, heads bent, the leading officer keeping a muffling hand over the mouth of Joseph Eley. The air became steadily more foul: breathing itself was a distasteful, sick-making effort. Daintree's mind raced, way ahead of his reaching feet: time! God, that was running out too fast! He fancied they must be nearing half way when the tunnel's downward slope began to flatten out; he wondered what would meet them at the farther end. They moved on, the tunnel floor now level. Midstream for sure... suddenly Daintree stumbled, nearly fell, nearly yelled obscenities. All that he in fact uttered was one four-letter word, under his breath.

In the next instant they all caught the loom of light from ahead, the up-and-down movement of a torch. Vague sounds came from Eley, whose mouth was still hand-silenced. The full beam of the torch lit the tunnel—whoever was coming had rounded a bend, a shallow bend no doubt dictated by some unyielding stratum beneath the river. Still far off, the beam had not, for the moment, shown up the police party.

Daintree ordered a halt.

The beam moved on. It would not be long now. A moment after they had halted, with Eley wriggling like a landed fish in the grip of the plain-clothes men, the beam moved to one side, shone on to a recess in the tunnel wall. Daintree saw outlined men, three men with guns dully reflecting the light from the torch: he recognized Cunliffe, Delabier and Massey.

Daintree gave the one order: 'Shoot to wound.'

Guns cracked out, sounding like heavy artillery. Pieces of muck dropped from the roof like rain. The police went forward at a crouching run, pushing Eley. There were cries, yells from the men ahead. Through gunsmoke, through a sharp stink of burnt powder, Daintree saw the flashes of the return fire. One of the men holding Eley spun and dropped, his head shattered, and Eley broke away in the confusion, ran blind into darkness, the torch now off. Daintree's men fired as blindly as they too ran on. Then, suddenly, came the very gates of hell: a massive explosion ahead, a brilliant light briefly flaring red and white and green, and filled with specks of blackness. Hot stinking air swept along the tunnel, blasting the police party flat. Daintree fell winded and gasping beneath a heavy body. Then something came down very hard on his exposed head and he passed out. He was not out for long: cold water followed the chunk of stone that had landed, no more than a glancing blow, on the side of his head. For half a minute he lay still, muzzy and sick, hardly registering. Then he felt the stir of bodies close by, the sounds of distress, the cries and moans of badly wounded men. And he became aware of rising water.

He staggered upright, hit his head again, felt sicker but took a grip. His torch was in a pocket: he fished for it. It worked still. The beam showed horror: three more of his men dead, two badly mauled. Just three no worse than he himself. And it showed the damage: the explosion-fractured tunnel roof, sagging, coming away, pouring Thames water mixed with mud and filth.

It showed, too, the totally blocked tunnel ahead.

Daintree felt drained of life, dared not look at his watch. In an old man's voice he said, 'On your feet ... those that can. Bring the wounded. Leave the dead for now. We're getting out,'back the way we came in. Cunliffe, Delabier and Massey ... they're the other side of that lot.'

He gestured ahead.

Carrying the wounded officers as best they could, they started back. It took them a long, long time and it exhausted what strength had been left to them by the appalling fug. The rising waters hastened them. They sloshed almost waist deep, with the wounded men's mouths only just clear of the filthy inflow. Somehow they made the rise of the tunnel floor and came a little clearer of the water. Then they saw the new lights ahead, the friendly lights of men who had heard the explosion and had come in to investigate.

* * *

Across the river in Rotherhithe, Cunliffe, Delabier and Massey emerged, shaken, with Joseph Eley and five gunmen. They were brought out, cautiously, quietly, from a low-set tidal exit similar to that on the Poplar side. They emerged on to another wharf, and were taken into another warehouse, this time one stacked high with merchandise—bales of wool, from Australia according to the markings. They were led in silence through gangways between the stacked bales, towards a door to the street, where a Bentley waited together with a $3\frac{1}{2}$-litre Rover. Into the Bentley went Cunliffe, Delabier and Massey, plus three armed guards. Into the Rover went Joseph Eley and two other men. At Eley's word, the cars moved off, heading east along the deserted road between high, grimy brick walls and buildings. Eley looked happy. But not for long: as the Bentley, gently purring, approached the end of the road, a police patrol nosed out to block it. In the Rover, Eley sat rigid, fists clenched tight. He yelled, unheard, towards the Bentley, 'Foot down, you bastard!'

No need to be yelled at: the Bentley's driver put his foot down and the big car surged forward powerfully. It took the police-car bumper and flung the vehicle aside with a scream of jagging metal and sliding rubber. Turning, Eley saw more patrols coming in behind from the other end of the dock road. Shouting at his own driver, Eley urged speed. They raced, swaying dangerously. With tyres screaming murder, they took corners following the Bentley, made Redriff Road, sped into Lower Road and on east for a while, then sharply turned right, taking the side-roads. They passed police in plenty—cars, motor-cycles. None of them stood in their track, not being suicidal. But the ring was closing fast. Eley had a fair run for his money until the end came in Greenwich, where the Bentley was faced, in a narrow street, by an empty Ford Escort parked slap across the exit. The driver tried to pass behind the Escort, and jammed up solid, with the Escort's rear bumper impaled into his offside front wheel and the Rover trying to climb into his boot. Joseph Eley's head hit the roof and his neck snapped. Police came out from cover, with guns, and closed in on Cunliffe, Delabier and Massey. Within three minutes, the words reached Daintree, en route for the Yard: 'Birds re-caged.'

The message was timed at fifteen minutes past midnight. By this time Daintree had been in contact with base, had been given the news of the extended deadline. He called the Commissioner back. 'Daintree. I'd like the birds taken direct, repeat direct, to the nearest RAF airfield. I'm flying them north. In the meantime, I'd advise immediate contact with the coach. Tell those terrorists we've got the bods.'

19

AT 01.50 hours Daintree and his prisoners landed at Edinburgh's Turnhouse airport by the Firth of Forth. Daintree came out at the rush, was met by a naval officer from Rosyth.

'I asked for a helicopter.'

'Ready and waiting. What d'you propose?'

'I'm heading for the bridge, and there's no time to lose. Can you contact the coach?'

'Yes—'

'Then tell them to hold everything, I'm on my way now. I'll make personal contact on arrival.'

'Right. By the way ... there are four helicopters moving in, picked up beyond Inchkeith.' The officer waved an arm. 'Unidentified, no markings. Kahn's escape route?'

Daintree said, 'Could be. We'll soon find out.' He paused, face set hard. 'Those television choppers. Still there, are they?'

'Yes—'

'Then get them cleared away. Quote any authority you like, just get rid of them. If they must ghoul, they can bloody well ghoul from long range.' He swung away and watched the transfer of the prisoners, under Pullen, to the naval helicopter. It was a fine, clear night, good hovering weather. Daintree climbed aboard and the entry hatch was shut. With a stomach-sinking sensation, the machine lifted and headed out, north and a little west. Very soon, the two bridges, rail and road, came into view below. Daintree surveyed the great structure of the road bridge as the pilot made for its centre, the collection of vehicles brilliantly lit by the searchlights. Then the pilot's shout: 'There they are ... the helicopters!'

Daintree saw them: one, centred over Kahn's strongpoint, was hovering, with its lifting cable winched down. As Daintree watched he saw a figure in what looked like a strait-jacket, a bulky form he fancied, being secured to the cable's end. He saw it lifted on the winch, up into the belly of the helicopter. As his own machine approached he saw the faces, upturned to watch. Someone waved; down once again came the cable, swinging a little, to be grappled in by the waiting hands below. When the winch took it up again, Daintree saw another man going up, holding two small children.

The pilot saw too. 'Kids,' he said wonderingly. 'The two from the dormobile they trapped?'

Daintree gave a nod. 'Kahn's in-flight hostages,' he said. 'The bastard! To ensure his safety . . . once he passes beyond the point of his remote control.' He went on staring down, assessing, wondering, a prey to all kinds of last-minute anxieties and doubts. He was running things very close, maybe too close. . . .

He reached for the microphone to make his contact with Kahn.

* * *

Harkness, some while earlier during the MacBean-led singing, had witnessed the lead-in to the last act, the lead-in of authority: another movement of police and military, this time back from the barricades at either end until, with a somehow furtive air as though they hoped the hostages hadn't seen them in spite of the brilliance of the illuminations, they had withdrawn right back to the approaches. It was more of a lead-out than a lead-in and it left nakedness behind it, a feeling of total desertion at the last. Below the bridge, the frigates also moved, going a little farther out to east and west. Likewise above: the air cover seemed to Harkness as he squinted upwards through the bars across his driving window, to be higher and no longer right overhead.

He thought: the bloody bastards! Not that he could really blame them: no point in more deaths. But surely, surely to God . . . at this last moment it would have been in order for the troops to mount a full-scale assault on the barricades and at least try to take Kahn's strongpoint?

Maybe they had something else up their sleeves, but Christ

... it was getting so bloody late! Harkness stared through the windscreen, thinking of Mary and the children.

* * *

Over the central position, now thankfully cleared of the intrusion of the television teams, Daintree hovered, looking down. Urgently he called Kahn on the radio. 'This is Commander Daintree of the Special Branch, overhead now. Hold everything, Kahn. We can talk, no rush. Over.'

He flicked his switch and waited, heart thumping hammerlike, blood pulsing past his eardrums, deafening. A long wait, then Kahtn's voice, almost amused. 'Talk, what about, Daintree? Over.'

Daintree was about to speak when the radio started playing up—interference, other voices. Somewhere, some bastard wasn't keeping his frequency clear. It seemed like utter confusion, but Daintree gathered something was being relayed to him. The Prime Minister's voice, strained to the point of desperation, back-pedalling hard now the birds had been actually retaken. 'There is to be no handover ... more talk I've promised, and a safe conduct ... no more, tell Daintree.' Then the Home Secretary, then the Commissioner—all yacking. Through it, Daintree flicked to transmit and spoke to Kahn.

'I have Cunliffe, Delabier and Massey. I have them here. Over.'

The reply, this time, came fast. 'Drop lower and show.'

Daintree nodded at the pilot. The helicopter sank, hovered low. Cunliffe, Delabier and Massey pressed faces to the glass of the ports, clearly visible in the searchlights. Kahn's voice came again, taut with excitement, with intense satisfaction: 'Okay, copper. What do you want?'

'I want to talk. Over.'

They waited: after an interval Kahn came up again: 'So talk. Make it fast. What are you offering, copper?'

'Safe conduct.'

'What's new in that?'

'It's your last chance, Kahn.'

'And the bloody coach passengers', plus.'

177

'I think not. For God's sake, man, see sense! Don't you value your own life?'

'My own life's in my own hands, copper. You attack, I blow—by remote control, or didn't they tell you?'

'They told me,' Daintree said into his microphone, voice shaking. 'They told me. Haven't you a conscience?'

'Go back to church,' Kahn said with a laugh. 'Raise the offer or I go off the air, finally. Over!'

Daintree's face streamed sweat. He looked at his pilot, looked down at the stranded coach, around at the escape helicopters hovering impudently, knowing they were safe. In one he could see the two young children—close at times, he could see their white, pinched faces, tear-stained, terrified. His mind projected down into the coach, visualizing the men and women inside. It was too much: the last risk had to be taken.

Daintree flicked his microphone alive. 'All right, Kahn. You can have them. Over.' He switched off, doing it with an air of finality, aware of startled reaction from Inspector Pullen. He shouted to the pilot, over the engine din, 'Can you go down really low and make a drop?'

'We'll winch them down, Commander.' The pilot passed his orders, brought the machine lower. The naval crew assembled at their stations, and opened the big bay ready as the helicopter dropped down to the bridge, swaying, lifting, settling in position. The pilot gave a signal: Cunliffe went first, shaking like a leaf. Then the other two. Daintree watched men running out to get them as the helicopter lifted again to hover in station some ninety feet clear of the carriageways. Into Daintree's ear, Pullen shouted, 'What now?'

'We wait. Wait for them to leave in the escape helicopters. In the meantime I'm going down. But not just here.'

* * *

The naval helicopter lifted higher, moved easterly and north, then turned in towards Inverkeithing. As it moved away, Kahn's escape fleet came in for the central area, hovering close. Daintree's radio began making vague noises again: a message from Defence Ministry—the aircraft from Hatherleigh had crossed the border into East Germany and the shadowing planes had detached. What the diplomatic moves were going to be Daintree could not estimate, and at this stage he didn't particularly care. He waited while his helicopter steadied over the northern bridge approach, over a staring crowd of troops and police and an assembly of vehicles. It came down, touching gently on the roadway, and Daintree got out with Pullen. As the helicopter lifted again with orders to shadow Kahn's escape, Daintree approached the brass, identified himself, and asked for ground transport and armed assistance.

'To do what?'

'I'm going in.' Daintree, outlined in brilliant light, pointed along the bridge. 'I've dropped Cunliffe, Delabier and Massey. Now I have to think about the hostages—'

'A handover's been expressly ruled out—'

'All the same,' Daintree broke in, 'it's been done. Now I have to make sure they don't get away—but first, the safety of the hostages. Are you going to help, Colonel?'

The colonel flapped. 'I don't understand—'

'It'll all come clear soon,' Daintree said soothingly. He looked around. 'Give me a personnel-carrier with a platoon of infantry and some sappers. And a radio expert. I'd like all the searchlights off—both ends, and from the frigates—' He broke off as he felt a hand on his arm. Turning, he faced a bearded man in jeans and a duffel coat. 'Yes?'

'The searchlights. We can't shoot in the dark, you know.'

'Shoot!' Daintree drew his sleeve across tired eyes. 'Who the bloody hell are you?'

'Outside Broadcast—'

'I'm sorry. The searchlights are going off and for all I care you can stuff all your cameras, one by one—'

'But look here, you can't interfere with—'

Daintree took the collar of the duffel coat in both his fists, and shook hard. He used two dismissive single-syllable words, and Outside Broadcasts took the hint. As the cameraman beat it, Daintree turned back to the colonel. *'Hurry, for God's sake hurry!'*

* * *

All set to go, Daintree gave the word to the Army driver. The personnel-carrier, with its troops and equipment embarked, moved forward for the southbound carriageway. Reaching it, Daintree swung round and gave a single flash on an Aldis lamp. At once the lights on the northern approach were cut, a fraction of a second later those from the southern entry and from the frigates went out together. There was a total blackness, a night-blindness that would last at any rate for a while—a blackness that would spoil the show for the millions of viewers watching the round-by-round broadcast from the shore-based cameras. Daintree took full advantage, hoping his driver would manage to keep safely on the carriageway in the first moments of night-blindness.

'Go!' Daintree shouted.

They went, fast towards the embattled centre, without lights of their own. The noise of the personnel-carrier's progress didn't worry Daintree too much: the din from the hovering helicopters was taking good care of that. Watching ahead, he could now see little: the light from the helicopters themselves was all the illumination left—that, and a faint glow, oblong-shaped, which could be from the rear window of the coach. But in the light from a helicopter immediately on station above the central area Daintree could see some activity, men being winched up into the belly of the machine. Anonymous men—too far off for any recognition. When Daintree had covered about half his distance, he saw the helicopter lift and another take its place, and more men go up.

His nerves jagged. Beside him Pullen, just a blur in the darkness, whistled softly through his teeth. Daintree hissed at him to shut up. Twenty yards short of the barbed wire, Daintree stopped the vehicle. The noise from the helicopters was intense now, and their downdraught could be felt strongly as they backed and filled overhead, waiting their turn to come in for the pick-up.

Another away: Pullen shouted into Daintree's ear. 'Do we wait till they're all gone, sir?'

'Yes. Then we move bloody fast. Be patient!'

It seemed an eternity before the next and last machine came in, seemed another age before the last of the hijackers was on the winch. From his nearer position now, Daintree believed he recognized Cunliffe, Delabier and Massey among that final consignment, followed by just one more man, who turned to give a wave towards the people in the coach: Kahn, the leader, last to leave?

Daintree looked upward, following the man into the hatch. The machine lifted, lurched a little, steadied, moved with the others easterly towards the entrance to the Firth of Forth, towards the North Sea. The naval helicopter, with its watching brief, turned in their wake, shadowing. Daintree wished it luck. He put a hand on Pullen's shoulder. 'Here we go,' he said. He turned to the men in the back, addressing a sergeant. 'All out....' He felt Pullen's hand, roughly, seizing his arm. 'What is it?'

'Fire, sir—fizzing. They've lit the fuse-trail!'

Daintree stared. He saw a redly-moving spark, spluttering along the carriageway, close to the coach. Daintree jumped down, ran for the barbed wire, took it, tore at it, ripping flesh, his head inflamed with fury at the hijackers... the spies gone, the bridge and its many lives still in jeopardy... *what was Kahn's idea?* He was throwing away his own immunity... then Daintree remembered the children aboard the helicopter. No-one would know which machine they were in, and all Kahn's fleet was safe. This final act was sheer sadism, a bastard's goodbye.

Daintree found men at his side. 'Leave it,' a voice said, the Army sergeant. The wire-cutters were at work. A gap was made and Daintree broke through, running for the fuse-trail. Reaching it, he took the flaring end in his hands and muffled it in the cloth of his jacket. Behind him, a soldier made certain by nipping off the wire.

'Radio,' Daintree said. 'Kahn's remote control. Any minute, he'll know the fuse hasn't worked!' He looked around, in a state approaching frenzy. 'Boot—that's where the explosive will be. *Get it bloody open!*'

He heard smashing sounds: the sergeant and two men were at work, not on the boot, but on the coach windows. Glass fell away and the sergeant spoke to Harkness, breathlessly: 'Keys of the boot, mate?'

'Gone. Kahn took them.' Harkness spoke in a dead flat voice. 'We've had it. Better get away.'

'Never say die.' The sergeant ran back to the boot, and started there with his two men, using axes and crowbars. Other men smashed away at the door of the coach, at its welded bolts. Blow after blow ... Daintree, watching helplessly, shook, every part of him urging them on. Only God knew, now, just how long they had. Daintree joined the sergeant at the boot: no luck, the metal was solid, was standing up to it, was still holding its terrible potential intact. Back with the sergeant to the door, past the faces at the windows, the pleading urgent faces of men and women.

'We're doing all right here,' the NCO said: the bolts were smashed away. Daintree took charge, mounting the steps into the coach. There was panic inside: they were all on their feet, shouting. Daintree lifted his voice in a roar: 'Take it easy, you're going to be all right. Out you come, one at a time.'

They rushed him like stampeded cattle. He was knocked down the steps, picked himself up, saw a man leap for the guardrail and drop down to the heavy steel beam below. He wasn't in time to stop the suicidal jump into the Forth, could only do what he could for the rest. He got in amongst the passengers, aided now by the troops, who used their fists when necessary. Once again Daintree lifted his voice: 'There's a gap in the north wire. Use it. Get through and run. Sergeant?'

'Sir?'

'The boot...'

'Looks fairly hopeless. Depends how much time we have.'

'Which we don't know. Can you clear away the barricades, both ends?'

'I reckon so—'

'Get to it, then. When they're sufficiently cleared, take the vans out north and south, pick up any of the passengers you find en route. Fast as you can!'

'Right, sir. And you?'

Daintree said, 'Me? I'm taking the coach off the bridge.' He was scarcely aware of the sergeant's incredulous look. He had a job to do, and the doing of it included the safety of the Forth road bridge. There could have been an element of atonement as well: he'd let the spies go, which was bad enough, perhaps, for national security. The sergeant went off, shouting orders, and men doubled towards the barbed wire. Daintree found Harkness back inside the coach, wearing his driver's cap and jacket—Harkness, ferreting about in the glove compartment.

'Driver?'

'Yes—'

'Get out, then, pronto.'

Harkness said defensively, 'There's a framed photo... my wife. I always take—'

'Leave it. You'll be seeing her soon—if you get out. Keys gone. I suppose?' The ignition was empty.

'Yes. What are you going to do?'

Daintree said once again, 'Take the coach off the bridge, what else? But maybe it's lucky I found you... can you start her for me?'

Harkness nodded. 'Sure I can. Now?'

'*Yes!*' Daintree trembled, wiped the sweat of cold fear from his face.

Harkness got back into his seat, brought some wire out from a pocket, a prudent reserve. He fiddled around with the ignition, behind the dash, got down and fiddled again in the engine compartment. The coach came alive. Harkness, back squarely in the driving seat, said, 'I'm used to her. I'll take her out. Leave it to me. I reckon you may be needed here.' He added, 'All along, right from the start, I've felt so bloody useless. Time I did something. It's my responsibility, you see. Not yours.'

Daintree said, 'Out. I'm in charge.' He turned as the sergeant ran past, going from the south barricade towards the northern one. He left the coach, ran up behind, calling out to the sergeant, who stopped.

Daintree said, 'Your radio section—'

'Yes?'

'Get them to send a message—Defence Ministry in London: Cunliffe, Delabier and Massey airborne, heading east with hijack party in four helicopters. All passengers clear—and I'm moving the coach out. Got that?'

'Yes, sir—'

'Tell them it's all clear for them to act—to mount a recovery operation. You'll have a code,' Daintree added. 'Use it. The message won't reach London before I'm clear of the bridge. All right?' From behind, he heard the sound of sudden movement. He swung round, ran hell for leather, south along the carriageway. With the doors slammed shut and all lights blazing, Harkness was on the move, fast, accelerating, steering into the overtaking lane to pass the removal vans, now shifted into single file to the left. Daintree fell behind, gasping, as the coach with its touch-and-go cargo in the boot crashed what remained of the barricade, burst through and on for the south approach.

20

KAHN was out over the North Sea now, well beyond Inchkeith, heading north-east in the general direction of Norway, his four escape helicopters keeping a close formation, and flying low, the pilots scanning the dark seas ahead. Cunliffe, Delabier and Massey, not yet able wholly to relax and enjoy freedom, sat together with Rubery and Kahn, astern of the leader which was carrying the final hostages. Away to starboard and a little behind came the shadowing helicopter of the Royal Navy. Higher, circling constantly, were watchful aircraft of the RAF, planes that had left the vicinity of the Forth road bridge when Kahn's helicopters had moved out.

Kahn had heard no explosion from the bridge but he saw no reason for worry.

* * *

The hands of driver Harkness gripped the wheel tightly, almost insanely, as he sent the coach hurtling down the carriageway for the southern approach. He was only dimly aware, as he came off the bridge itself, of the staring crowds of troops and police, of the vehicles being driven fast out of his rushing headlights. With his foot hard down he roared Tour Eighteen through the approach area, stormed on to the A90, the road for Edinburgh. He felt light-headed, a mixture of sheer relief that he was out of the hands of Kahn and Kerrigan and Silver, that his passengers were safe at last; and of an acute awareness of his personal danger. Sweat poured down his face, but he hardly noticed. Behind his headlight beams he drove on, foot still hard down, the coach rocking and swaying, veering to the centre and back again, driven harder than it had ever been driven before. He could not stop yet, he told himself. He must not block the main highway from the bridge with a massive explosion. In his rear-view mirror he saw the empty interior of the coach, still dimly lit, still with its paraphernalia of personal belongings—hand cases, bags, cameras and the like—reminders. Old Hanborough was in his mind: Hanborough would have approved of him now, taking a soldier's view. Harkness was sorry about the old man's terrible end. He thought about others; Hanborough's wife, Brewster and Hurst, young Larcombe, Susan Larcombe who had never regained her speech—but there was time for that, now.

He drove on, his mind racing with the coach. Somehow, he felt unable to stop. His duty was not yet done.

* * *

In the wake of Harkness, Daintree reached the southern bridge approach.

'The coach?'

'Passed through, no explosion. That driver's a hero.'

'You can say that again.' Daintree mopped at his face with a handkerchief. Harkness deserved a medal—he would see that he got something in the nature of one. Daintree, borrowing a radio-equipped police car, left the approach, heading out fast behind Harkness. No sign of the coach. After some minutes, his radio called him.

'Daintree, over.'

'OC Troops at bridge. Response from Defence Ministry: with airborne hostages in mind, they're ordering no direct attack. Cover aircraft are ordered to buzz Kahn intensively and shepherd his fleet in westerly, towards Aberdeen. Over.'

'Aberdeen airport?'

The voice crackled. 'We don't expect miracles, but we're hoping to bring them down there under pressure. We're going to get them, and in the last resort—if Kahn does use the hostages—we'll have to press it home. Is there anything you want, from your end? Over.'

Daintree thought quickly, as his driver took him on behind Harkness. 'I'm turning back, heading for Aberdeen.' He had to be in at the kill, had now to leave the coach to Harkness. 'Remember the coach driver, please. Has Defence Ministry informed Kahn his big stick's broken? Over.'

'No. Once he knows that, the airborne hostages are in greater danger. One more thing: there'll be no television teams at Dyce. Over and out.'

Daintree felt sickened as, to his order, the police driver took the car back towards the bridge, from the roundabout east of South Queensferry. Children were children... no argument, you had to go to the limit. Pendennis was Pendennis, Pendennis was a general. *And Harkness?* Daintree deliberately forced down thoughts of Harkness: nothing he could do would alter anything now. Driving fast, no drop of speed for bridge limits, Daintree's car crossed the Forth to the north approach, swept past the clustered ex-passengers who were being given food and hot drinks, into the Kingdom of Fife, taking the A90 for Milnathort and Perth towards the A94 for Stonehaven—a long drive, but the roads in the early hours were nicely clear. Daintree slumped in his seat, tried to sleep but found his mind too actively orientated towards the drama out over the North Sea. Those buzzing, close-flying fighters, the naval helicopters... Kahn's reactions, the reactions of a man seeing the net draw in so unexpectedly. Probably he had been heading for a sea rendezvous, a merchant ship maybe, equipped with a platform for landing-on helicopters. Safe behind his hostages, his threat of the big blow-up, he would be, or would have been until now, cocking snooks at the shadowing force. And now? Daintree's thoughts curdled: one radio signal from Kahn's remote control apparatus, and Harkness would fragment.

Other matters took Daintree's mind off Harkness: he was being kept fully in the picture by his two-way radio. At Perth the word came that Kahn had been turned, all four of his helicopters heading westerly for the Scottish coast. Every effort would be made to head him in for Aberdeen's airport at Dyce. Assuming he could be forced to land somewhere, it was hoped at least that it would be in the vicinity of Dyce. To receive him, held under cover, would be a strong force of police, plus a Scottish infantry battalion, plus fire engines and ambulances nearby: but all Kahn would see on his arrival would be the empty airfield and its buildings...

'It won't help,' Daintree said to his driver. 'He'll kill the hostages—the children.'

'That may not be so, sir. They're his last card, are they not?'

'Yes...'

'I've a feeling he'll hang on, sir. We just have to be faster, that's all.'

Daintree looked sideways. 'Use guns, kill him first—and Cunliffe, Delabier and Massey?'

'What would you do, sir?'

Daintree laughed; a grim laugh. 'Point taken!' He said no more. A little way out of Perth another message came in, not unexpectedly: there had been a shattering explosion reported from a minor road running south from Barnton, the other side of the A9, beyond Currie towards the Pentland Hills. Harkness had taken his coach well clear. Investigation had revealed devastation on and around the roadway with fragmented coach sections spread extensively over open country. There had been no sign of the driver, but there had been blood spattered over the broken metalwork.

* * *

Daintree reached Dyce at a few minutes past 05.00, after a furious piece of driving. The sky, still dark, was stormy, heavy with rain and lowering cloud but otherwise apparently empty. Daintree, grateful at least for the absence of the television crews, stayed in the open after a word with the police and the military: pacing, pacing, scanning those empty skies as slowly they lightened with the dawn, cold, hungry, dead tired but totally unable to relax. Upon arrival he had been met by cold words from London: the Prime Minister was appreciative of salvation for the coach party and the bridge, but otherwise strongly condemned Daintree's flouting of his wishes.

Daintree was on a knife-edge: retirement loomed close. Quite apart from this aspect, he was sick inside at the thought that Cunliffe, Delabier and Massey might well get away with it. Also Kahn, who had killed Harkness. Daintree conferred with the local police: there were, they told him, not a few places where Kahn could decide to ditch. It hadn't got to be Dyce.

'And if not?'

A shrug: 'Wherever it is, we have local forces who'll cope.'

'Not foolproof, is it?' Daintree bit his nails.

'We're not able to cover everywhere, not all the time, but we have plenty of mobility.'

'Let's bloody hope it's right here at Dyce,' Daintree said savagely. He waited, waited... looking and pacing still, hoping, praying. Then, at 06.23 hours precisely, the word came through, a message received from the shadowing leader via Defence Ministry: 'Helicopters approaching coast likely to cross inwards close south of Balmedie.'

Daintree asked, 'Balmedie?'

'Some ten miles off us, north-easterly.'

Daintree went on waiting. He felt better now: so far, so good. At least they were coming back to Scotland.

* * *

Prayer it seemed worked: the helicopters made Dyce spot on. The skill and determination of the shadowing pilots forced Kahn in where they wanted him, where the civil and military powers were known to be ready to take him. Daintree watched from his cover, watched the first approach of the machines, with the RAF fighters swooping, crossing, cutting in, forcing the escape fleet in to touchdown. It was grotesque, incredible, a masterly performance. Down and down, swaying, lifting, veering from side to side, pitching noses, reluctant landers... Daintree felt the sweat run cold, wondered which machine contained the hostages. Down over the airport buildings... down, down... then sudden emergency: one of the machines, under too close a pressure perhaps, misjudged. Its wheel touched a roof, it lurched, caught its rotor-blades. It toppled, completely out of control, bounced a little, rising on a gust of wind, slewed sideways, then fell back with a crash on the roof and rolled down to the ground.

Flames licked and curled.

Daintree, shaking, gave the order to wait. 'The rest down first.' He felt physically sick with a terrible fear. Praying that the children might not be in the burning helicopter, he watched, waited, his nerves hammering. The other machines touched: still the fighters roared low across the airfield, beating at it with waves of sound, speeding across, then turning to come in again.

Daintree shouted, '*Now!*'

He ran out himself, ready to kill if need be. The whole airfield erupted with men, armed men who ran to surround the escape fleet. The fire-fighting vehicles roared into life. Foam poured whitely over the burning helicopter, too late: it was reduced already to redly-glowing framework in which, horribly, could be seen the outlines of bodies, pouring melted fat. *Whose?* Daintree looked away, unable to take it. When he ran across to make the arrest of Kahn in person, and Kerrigan, and Silver and many more, he passed his gun to a uniformed constable, knowing that if it was in his hand he would use it to kill.

* * *

'Rest,' the Commissioner said. 'That's what you need. Get it. That's an order.' The Commissioner had come in by air with other V.I.P.'s shortly after it was all over. 'I don't want you collapsing on me.'

'I'll not do that,' Daintree said. He felt numb, as though he would never be the same again. When the hostages had been brought out from their helicopter, safe and sound, he had all but broken down: that was unpolicemanlike, but he hadn't felt very policemanlike. There was a lot of sorting out to do, trying to make out who was dead, for one thing. The redelivery of three spies to gaol was another. Then the interrogation of the surviving hijackers, an investigation into the associations of Joseph Eley... Daintree said, 'I need a very strong whisky, sir.'

'I thought you might. Here.' The Commissioner produced a flask. Daintree took a deep pull. It helped. The Commissioner gave him a close look. 'It's complete success,' he said wonderingly. 'Yet you look as though you failed. Why?'

Daintree said, 'A man called Harkness. That's why.'